PASSION IN
FLAMES

CAROLYN WREN

Serenity Press

Copyright © 2018 Carolyn Wren

First published as *The Scientist* in 2013 by Secret Cravings Publishing
Published by Serenity Press in 2018

All rights reserved. No part of this book may be used or reproduced by any means, graphic, electronic, or mechanical, including photocopying, recording, taping or by any information storage retrieval system without the written permission of the copyright owner except in the case of brief quotations embodied in critical articles and reviews.

This is a work of fiction. Names, characters, businesses, places, events and incidents are either the products of the author's imagination or used in a fictitious manner. Any resemblance to actual persons, living or dead, or actual events is purely coincidental.

National Library of Australia Cataloguing-in-Publication data:
Passion in Flames/Serenity Press
Romance – fiction

ISBN: (sc) 978-0-6483116-7-6
ISBN: (e) 978-0-6483317-0-4

Serenity Press books may be ordered through online booksellers or by contacting: publisher@serenitypress.org

SERENITYPRESS.ORG

Serenity Press

When I wrote Notes of Desire, I didn't plan on writing a series, until Simon Winters charmed his way into readers' hearts. This book is for the Simon fans, who wanted his story.

Chapter 1

Perfection. These days, that term was used for everything from coffee to selfies.

Beth had her own definition more suited for such an elegant word. To her, perfection was the tiny, unique world visible only through the lens of a powerful microscope. In fairness, today's example was more blurry haze than perfect. She could fix that. Beth made an infinitesimal adjustment with the tip of her finger to the lever on her left, teasing the image into focus. The familiar rush of anticipation sent a flood of energy through her body as she scrutinised the strands of fibres pressed between the slides. The uniformity of the magnified textile was flawless, utterly free from defects or weak spots.

'Yes!' She gave herself a mental high five. 'Test A4D3 completed successfully. Another home run for Team Barrett.'

Beth jumped as something brushed her arm, jarring the image back to a blur.

'Sorry. I didn't mean to startle you.' Tim, her lab assistant, removed his hand with an apologetic smile.

She squinted at him, blinking in the sudden light and at the unwelcome need to refocus on reality. 'It's okay. Is something wrong?'

'It's seven-thirty pm. I wondered if you needed anything from me before I left.'

Beth glanced around, noting with some surprise the encroaching darkness through the windows, and the emptiness of the laboratory. *Time flies when you're having fun.* 'It's fine, Tim, go home. I'll lock up.'

His smile widened. '*You* go home at some point too, Dr Barrett.'

'I will. I promise.' The reassurance was automatic. The other technicians were always badgering her to broaden her horizons, to party. Their favourite quote was something about redheads and passion. Beth had no idea what her hair colour had to do with her personality. Furthermore, she had no desire to party, and liked her horizons exactly where they were. The fleeting musings came and went. She was already refocusing her microscope, oblivious to anything else.

A sound penetrated her concentration sometime later, and Beth lifted her head, wincing as the muscles in her neck protested the sudden movement. 'Hello?' Silence answered her. The moon had chased away the remaining daylight, leaving the spacious room in almost complete darkness, apart from the microscope's built-in light.

There. A faint tinkling came from along the corridor. Beth suppressed a shiver of fear. Had she locked the doors after Tim left? Her intentions had been good, but as usual her work had taken control, stealing away the hours without her even realising it.

Another sound echoed the first. Footsteps. Slow, cautious, stealthy. Beth swallowed the lump in her throat. *Stop being an idiot. One of the lab assistants probably forgot something.* Her trepidation increased when she saw the beam bobbing in time with the almost silent footfalls. *A lab assistant would turn on the main lights. They wouldn't use a flashlight.*

Rising from her desk, holding the chair still to stop its customary squeak, she peered through the door into the dim corridor. The light swept back and forth in a searching arc. Beth peeked at the lamp on her desk. The circle of light was small, but visible. Turning it off now would only alert the intruder to her presence. Moving to another desk further along the wall, she crouched behind it and waited.

A silhouetted figure crossed the threshold into the lab. Beth held her breath as her heart thudded like a drum in her chest. Sure enough, the intruder headed to her desk and the light coming from her equipment. Beth hunkered further down, trying to fold her body into an inconspicuous ball even though the action blocked her view of the room and its unwanted occupant.

Noises came from the desk. Rustling, tinkling sounds, and the wooden creak of drawers being opened and closed. After a few torturous minutes, the shadowy figure began to move away. Beth's captured breath whooshed out of her laboured lungs in relief. *Shall I make a run for it?* No, better to wait until they left the building entirely. Beth put a hand to her chest. Her heart was hammering so hard she was afraid the intruder would hear it and come back.

One minute passed, then another. Surely they'd gone by now? A cough made her jump and look around in alarm. Something was tickling her throat, an acrid chemical smell wafting into her nostrils. Beth bit back another cough, holding her hands to her face, and peered over the top of the desk.

The area appeared brighter, and Beth could see why. Fire was racing along the corridor, creating its own light as it went.

My work, my microscope!

With no thought of the intruder, and no thought for her safety, Beth scrambled from her hiding place and sprinted to her desk, slamming her ankle into a table leg in her haste. She grabbed a cardboard box of recycled paper from underneath and dumped the contents on the ground. Scooping up her prized microscope, she shoved it inside, wincing as something cracked ominously in complaint of the rough treatment. She lost precious seconds gathering up her files and samples and rummaging for her keys. Her fingers shook as she fumbled with them, searching for the right one *and* the location of the cupboard keyhole by touch alone. She'd almost given up altogether when the key surrendered its struggle and slid into the lock with ease. The cupboard door hit the wall with a bang as she wrenched it open. Beth had no time to worry about the noise alerting any leftover trespassers. She snatched up her hard drive and added it to the box. *What else? What else can I save?* The frantic thought was made redundant as a hacking cough rattled her chest. How had the smoke gotten so thick so fast? Beth fumbled her way to the door. Firelight flared in both directions. She stood frozen, the box clutched in her hands. *How am I going to get out?*

The firelight seemed dimmer to the left, making the decision easier. The heat hit her as soon as she entered the corridor. Beth coughed again, wiping tears from her eyes as they blinded her progress. Forcing herself to stop, she squinted, disorientated by the smoke, dancing flames and her increasing fear. *Am I going to die here?* A shadow appeared in front of her, seizing her upper arm. Beth gasped, almost collapsing as the action drew searing-hot air into her lungs.

Another figure joined the first, and through her streaming tears she saw the mask of a fireman. In an effort to hold her upright, he tried to remove the box from her hands. She shook her head and clutched it to her chest. She staggered, half blinded and woozy. He wrapped his arm around her waist, dragging her from the smoke-filled building.

The fresh air outside was cold on her skin, a blessed chill that caused fresh tears to blur her vision even further. She flinched when something was held over her face, relaxing as a welcome rush of oxygen streamed from the plastic mask and into her lungs. A concerned paramedic draped a blanket around her shivering body. A second tried to remove the box from her clutching fingers. Beth resisted, and they shrugged, continuing their examination.

Through the open ambulance doors, she saw the smoke billowing from her laboratory windows, felt the spray of the cold, high-pressure water emitting from the fire hoses.

'You were lucky, ma'am,' a fireman said. 'There's a can of petrol by the back door. Semi-industrial areas like this are prone to vandalism.' He walked away, murmuring something about bored teenagers.

Visions scampered through her mind, of careful, stealthy footsteps, the intruder rummaging through her desk.

This was no adolescent act of vandalism.

Someone had tried to burn down her lab, with her inside it.

※

Simon Winters tilted the visitors' chair back on its two back legs until he found the sweet spot, and propped his legs up on the desk, feet crossed at the ankles, knowing just how much the act would annoy the man in front of him. 'I'm bored.'

Jared Knight glanced up from his paperwork just long enough to give him a long-suffering frown. 'You can't be bored. You just returned from an assignment.'

'The *nightmare* assignment, you mean. You have no idea of the hell I went through. For three weeks, I dragged that informant through the desert to safety. Three tortuous weeks and all he did was complain. The sun was too hot. The nights were too cold. He was thirsty. Seriously, I considered giving him back to the bad guys.'

Jared ran his gold pen through his fingers. 'Considering you survived a month in a war zone, you don't appear to have suffered any significant personal injury.'

Simon held out his arm. 'I'm sunburnt.'

'I'll add aloe vera oil to your expense claim. If you're bored, you can help me with this lot.'

'Paperwork? You want me to do *paperwork*?' Simon's look of horror brought an unwilling smile to Jared's face. Breaking through his friend's stoic façade was one of Simon's favourite pastimes.

'Administration and book-keeping are necessary.'

'A necessary evil, you mean. What's in those folders that has you so interested, anyway?'

Jared slid a pile across the desk. 'I'm compiling a list of agents currently incapacitated.'

'Are there that many?'

'Last month was chaotic. If this list gets any longer, we'll have to hire more people.'

Simon snagged the top one and started reading. 'Peter has concussion again? Good god, that man's a magnet for fallen or thrown objects.'

'He's lucky. The explosion was massive. His injuries could have been considerably worse. Omega's out of action too, our second concussion for the month. She's been ordered to rest for the next few weeks.'

'Do you think she'll obey doctor's orders?'

'Who knows, and we have no way of checking. And, lastly, there's Bryce. As you know, he's on the inactive list.'

Simon pushed the folders aside and resumed his gravity-defying position on the chair. 'Jet won't mind the downtime. He'll hibernate in that hermit house of his and build something ridiculously complex.'

Jared neatened the messy pile and tugged a wrinkled sheet of paper from under Simon's shoes. 'Until we find some new agents, you can pick up the mission slack.'

'Fine, as long as it's a fun mission.'

'Define fun.'

Simon tapped his chin in thought. 'I don't know. A beautiful woman in mortal peril, maybe?'

'Anything else on your wish list?'

'A fast car would be nice.'

'You do understand the object of our assignments is to *save* our clients, not seduce them, or put them in further danger.'

'I'm crushed, *crushed*, that you think me so shallow.' Simon's affronted tone was met with another half-smile.

The familiar banter was interrupted by Jared's PA, who strode in juggling two mugs of steaming tea and a file tucked under her arm. She sidestepped Simon's attempt to steal one of the drinks. 'If you're so bored, get your own. You know where the kitchen is.'

Simon gave her a mock glare. 'Do you always listen in on people's private conversations?'

She threw him a wink in return. 'It's part of my job, Blue Eyes.'

Jared held out his hand for the file. 'What's this?'

'Hot off the press. An assignment for an underworked, overpaid, thrill-seeking, danger junkie. Trust me, it's perfect.'

Jared flipped open the folder and scanned the first page. This time his smile was broad and genuine. 'Simon, I'm about to make your day.'

Beth took her first deep lungful of fresh air not tinged with the smell of hospital anaesthetic. Her abused lungs objected and her breath hitched. She couldn't believe they'd kept her in the ward overnight. Despite her continuous insistence of being fine, it appeared hospital protocol could not be overruled. A barrage of tests, a full physical examination later and she was finally free. *Not that I have any urgent tasks that require my attention.* Her breath hitched for a different reason. Her lab was a singed mass of smoke, a water-damaged crime scene.

Beth clasped the smoke-stained box to her chest, juggling it with the 'get well soon' oversized flower arrangement on top. The nurses had given up trying to remove the box from her room and locked it into the cabinet beside her bed, even taping it up when she asked. There'd been no opportunity to check the microscope for damage. She could only hope everything had escaped unscathed. She'd run a full diagnostic as soon as she got home. The thought of being productive buoyed her mood.

Gazing around the car park, Beth tried to spot her ride. The only information she had was a brief phone message from Haden Corporation saying someone would collect her. The words 'personal protection' had been used during the conversation. Beth was trying to block that part out. Where was he? Shouldn't punctuality be a given for a bodyguard? The only people in the immediate vicinity were a family loading a woman in a wheelchair into a van and an exceptionally tall blond man walking away from a black sports car.

Beth rolled her shoulders to ease the tension in her neck. She was desperate for a hot bath and a change of clothes, and to unwind in the peace and quiet of her own house.

Out of the corner of her eye, she saw blondie heading her way. *No, please, no flirting. I'm not in the mood.* Men tended to flirt with Beth. She never understood why, and never knew how to respond.

'Hi.' The man held out his hand.

'Hi.' Beth ignored the gesture.

One finely shaped brow rose. 'I don't think you understand. I'm—'

'No thanks.' She walked away, scanning the area for her recalcitrant protector, and jerked at the firm tap on her shoulder.

'I think there's been some misunderstanding. I'm the person you're waiting for.'

Did that pick up line ever work for him? 'Don't be ridiculous.' Beth shifted the weight in her arms and turned her back.

A second tap had her spinning around, just in time to see her golden-haired stalker put a ringing phone on top of the flowers and walk away, leaning against the car with a languid grace, arms folded.

Beth stared at the phone before lifting it to her ear with more than a little trepidation. 'Hello?'

The masculine voice on the other end was deep and calm. 'Dr Barrett, my name is Jared Knight. I've been asked to clarify something for you.'

Beth lowered the phone a minute later, forgetting even to disconnect the call. She stole a peep at the Adonis still watching her. He lifted his hand in a jaunty wave.

This ... blond playboy is my bodyguard?

His expression changed in a heartbeat from mischievous to intense. Without warning, he sprinted toward her, his long legs eating up the space in a microsecond. Beth yelped as strong arms snapped around her and swung her to the footpath, just as a dark-coloured car roared past, missing them by inches. She could only stare, dumbfounded, as it sped off into the distance.

Those muscular arms kept her ensnared, even as he tracked the car's progress. A cardboard corner was digging into her ribs and the fragrance of battered flowers rose in the air. A muttered curse under his breath told her his identification attempt had been unsuccessful and his expression relaxed when he pulled his attention back to her.

'Hi. Shall we start over? Simon Winters at your service.'

Her heart was making a valiant attempt to escape through her throat as she tried to regain the power of speech. 'You're crushing my box.'

'Pardon?' He peered at the cardboard and floral barrier between them. 'Ah, right. For a moment I thought – never mind. Tell me, do you always live such an exciting life?'

'No.'

A grin lit up his already handsome features. 'That's a shame. I like a bit of excitement. Come on, Red, let's get you home.'

Beautiful. Gorgeous. Breathtaking. Beth ran out of superlatives. Where was a thesaurus when you needed one? She snuck another furtive peek as Simon curved the powerful car into a sharp corner.

She was five-eleven. He had to be six-four or more, with sky blue eyes and movie star features, all framed by sun-streaked blond hair. A bodyguard? Seriously? She would have guessed male model or actor. With his skin kissed by a recent dose of the sun, he could have even been a professional athlete on a break from competition. His accent was another surprise, pure upper class British. This man would be at home in a glittering ballroom surrounded by society's finest. Was that suit custom made? The black jacket had been consigned to the back seat, leaving him wearing a crisp grey shirt with an open collar over the matching trousers and ridiculously shiny black shoes. Every tall inch of him was a study in stylish elegance. Beth knew little about clothes. She had a feeling her new bodyguard knew a *lot*. Her mind took an interesting tangent, imagining him on the cover of a romance novel, set in Regency times, wearing one of those cutaway jackets with buff-colored skin-tight trousers over his—

The blue gaze collided with hers, and she jumped at being caught ogling.

'Are you feeling okay? You look a little dazed.'

'Fine, fine, I'm … fine.' When had English become her second language?

"How's the ankle? Do you need anything? Prescriptions? We can stop on the way home.'

'The hospital gave me sleeping pills. I don't want to take them. How did you know about my ankle?'

'I read your medical report. You should consider the pills, even if it's just for a night or two. Traumatic situations can have side effects. You're probably tenser than you realise.'

'I'm fine, really.'

He gestured to her lap. 'You're clutching that cardboard so tight your knuckles are white.'

'I'm looking forward to getting home, that's all.'

'Okay.'

'That's it, okay?'

'I know about the importance of home.'

She didn't have an answer for that. Another thought struck her as he turned onto the highway. 'I didn't tell you where I live.'

Simon threw her a mischief-filled wink. 'I know everything about you. I have a file.' He removed the folder tucked into his seat and handed it to her.

'Everything?'

Another wink and a wide grin. 'Pretty much.'

'Why does the file have a sticky note on the front that says *behave*?'

'Jared has an odd sense of humour.'

'The man from the phone?'

'That's him.'

'He's your boss?'

'He does the paperwork we all hate. Listen, Red, I have a question.'

'About the fire?'

'Your job. Head researcher at age twenty six. You must have been a child prodigy?'

Beth's hackles rose at the all too familiar remark. 'I worked very hard to get where I am.'

'I meant it as a compliment, not an insult.' He carried on, not waiting for a response. 'The research you're doing is important enough to hire someone like me, and I don't come cheap.'

I bet you don't. 'Mr Haden said he was concerned for my welfare. I'm a practical person, Mr Winters, I'm certain their concern stems more from the significant financial potential of my work. My research is a matter of pride to *me*.'

'Simon, it's just Simon, and again, I meant no insult. I'm trying to put the facts together.' He took one hand off the wheel to squeeze her fingers. His suntanned skin was warm, and a vivid contrast to her pale coloring. 'If you turn to the police report, you'll see the fire has been ruled as a burglary.'

'That's what I was told.' *And I don't agree.*

'I don't agree.' Her words echoed back to her in his voice.

'Why not?'

'Numerous reasons.' He continued to watch her, a powerful intelligence lurking behind those baby blue eyes.

She jerked a finger at the windscreen. 'Could you please watch where you're going?'

That grin came back in full force. 'Sorry, yes.'

He agreed with her? That simple statement calmed some of the turbulent thoughts running around her mind since she sat in that ambulance and watched the billowing smoke.

'Music?'

'Sorry?'

'Would you like to listen to some music? Press that button, find a station you like.'

His quick-fire mood changes were impossible to follow. Beth gave up trying. She found a station playing light classical music and sank back against the butter-soft leather seats, thinking about that warm bath and the comforts of home.

She woke from a light doze as he pulled the car into her driveway.

Simon turned to her. 'I don't suppose I can convince you to go to a hotel with me?'

'What?' The single word came out louder than she'd intended.

'A hotel. They're much easier to secure. Footmen on the doors. Cameras in the halls. That sort of thing.'

'Oh, oh, of course.' Beth willed the heat from her cheeks. 'No, I don't want to go to a hotel. This is my home.'

'I didn't think so. Your file says you're stubborn.'

'Does it?'

Wow, that grin of his was addictive. 'Nope, I made that bit up. Please wait here while I do a spot check.'

He strode up her driveway and the few steps to her house, glancing right and left as he went. With hands shoved into his pockets, he was the epitome of casual. Was that part of his 'act'? Did bodyguards have an act?

Producing a key from his pocket, he let himself inside, bringing her hyperactive ponderings to an abrupt halt. Why did he have a key?

After a few minutes, he returned and opened her car door. 'All clear.'

'How did you get a key to my house?'

'I didn't. I broke in last night. You had *dreadful* security, by the way. I arranged to get the locks changed. Don't look so shocked. My job is to keep you safe. If I can break in, someone else can. It's all part of the service.'

He held the car door open and she alighted, keeping a wary eye on him, not sure about this tall, blond, gorgeous creature who seemed very unlike a bodyguard.

Beth stepped through the front door, letting the calm normality of home seep into her bones. Not an easy feat with Simon keeping up a line of chatter behind her.

'Considering its age, I like your house. It's eclectic.'

'Is that your way of saying nothing matches?'

'What I said, eclectic.'

She liked her house too. She'd spent a long time and a lot of money renovating the Victorian cottage in her personal style and was pleased with the result, from the modern kitchen to the vintage serenity of the master bedroom. *Has Simon been in my bedroom?*

'Have you lived here long?'

Beth turned to face him, an unwilling smile making her lips twitch. 'Isn't that in my file?'

'Yes, I was making conversation. Back in a moment.'

He disappeared back down the driveway. Beth closed her eyes, relishing the silence. It was *so* good to be home. The events of yesterday were easier to put behind her when she was here, surrounded by her things.

Okay, let's get organised. Squaring her shoulders, she put the box and the battered flowers on the kitchen table. Her stomach had started rumbling the moment she'd crossed the threshold. Hospital meals left much to be desired, and her return home seemed to have stimulated her appetite as well as her sense of well-being.

Simon shouldered open the front door as she was contemplating her food options. In one hand he had a brown bag with vegetables sticking out of the top and in the other a wheeled suitcase.

'Essentials.' He handed her the groceries. 'I wasn't sure what you liked, so I got all the basics. I'll put this away.' He gestured to the case and started for her spare bedroom.

'Put what away?' She followed him, the bag still in her arms.

'My clothes.' He was unpacking, unfolding, and hanging a remarkably large amount of apparel into the chest of drawers and wardrobe as if he did it every day.

'The chicken will start to drip if you don't get that into the fridge soon.' He pointed to the bag. 'I'll finish up here and start lunch. I'm sure you want to shower and change.'

He can't possibly mean ...

'You're living here?' she blurted out the question after a beat of stunned silence, alarmed to hear her voice rise in pitch. 'With me?'

'Of course.' He shook out a fine cotton shirt. 'How else am I meant to protect you?' Picking up a toiletries bag, he headed across the hall. 'Only one bathroom? How cosy.' He turned and gave her a smile hot enough to melt the world's polar ice caps.

Beth's feeling of peace and serenity at being home started to evaporate.

Shoving aside the clamouring thoughts in her head, she put the food away and fled to the bathroom. The small space was even smaller with his array of toiletries lining her mirrored shelf. The longed-for hot bath was sacrificed in favour of a quick shower. Peeking out the door, wrapped in her bathrobe, she made an undignified dash to her bedroom and flung on fresh jeans and a jumper.

Delicious smells coming from the kitchen lured her. She ventured forth, still rubbing her hair with a towel.

'Better?' Simon was chopping tomatoes with all the flare of a top chef.

'Much. You don't have to cook.'

'Yes, I do.' He placed a grilled chicken salad with gourmet feta cheese and a spicy dressing in front of her at the dining table and took a spot opposite. He'd even arranged the hospital flowers in a vase.

Sheer hunger dispelled any awkwardness. Beth put aside her qualms about her bizarre new living arrangement and tucked in.

Gesturing with his fork, he pointed to the battered, smoke-stained box. 'What's in there?'

'Work.'

'Okay.' Simon went back to his food.

'That's it? *Okay?*'

He nodded. 'I understand secrets, Elizabeth.'

'So you *do* know my name.'

The already familiar grin returned. 'Of course, it's in your file. People call you Beth. I happen to think Red suits you much better. What are you wearing?'

Beth stared at her clothes in confusion. 'Sorry?'

'To the awards dinner tomorrow night, remember? Big fancy restaurant in London?'

She'd completely forgotten. 'After everything that's happened, I don't think I'll go.'

'Nonsense. Of course you're going. People don't get awards for scientific achievement every day. I brought something suitable to wear. I promise not to embarrass you.'

Beth had a vision of her colleagues' reaction when she walked into the restaurant with a tuxedo-clad Simon on her arm. She smiled, taking her empty plate to the sink.

'See? You're looking forward to it already. What are you wearing?'

'To be honest, I have no idea. Fashion isn't my thing. I have a black dress in my wardrobe. I guess that'll do.'

'Hmm.' He gave her a thorough perusal from head to toe.

Beth had a sudden urge to cover herself with her hands. 'What does *hmm* mean?'

'It means hmm.'

'That *isn't* an answer.'

'What's the award for?'

Beth had the usual trouble following his rapid-fire changes of subject. 'Mould.'

His brows shot up. 'Mould?'

'*'The benefits of mould in a modern-day ecosystem'* if you want the full title. It's a fascinating subject.'

An exaggerated shudder shook Simon's long-limbed frame. 'I'll take your word for it.' He leaped to his feet with that lightning-fast energy she was already getting used to. 'Given your preference for mouldy things, maybe I should do the dishes.'

Beth stuttered in outrage until she saw the gleam of amusement on his face. 'You're teasing me.'

He tugged at a damp curl hanging over her shoulder. 'Yes, am I forgiven?'

'Are you always this wicked?'

'Guilty as charged. Do you have anything important to do tonight?'

Beth gave the box a wistful peep.

'It was a rhetorical question. Work is out of the question. You only got out of the hospital today.'

He was right. Surrounded by the comforts of home, and with good food in her stomach, fatigue was starting to make its presence known.

'Go to bed before you collapse where you stand. I need to make some calls, so I'll stay up for a while.' He took her hands and turned her toward the bedroom with a small push at her back. 'I'm here. You can relax now.'

Beth had some reservations about that statement, but fatigue won out and she was too tired to argue. Funny though, she could still feel the warmth of his touch minutes later as she tumbled into a dreamless sleep.

ଞ

Simon swung his legs over the bed and stretched, groaning as his spine spasmed in complaint. Although his initial survey of Beth's home had revealed two bedrooms, he'd guessed the sofa bed in the spare room would be neither large enough nor comfortable. Unfortunately, he'd been right on both counts, and anticipated a few more painful nights.

The sounds of running water reached him from across the hall even though dawn was only just breaking. His sexy scientist was making sure to avoid any damp, half-dressed confrontation in the hallway. It didn't stop his imagination from wandering, picturing water cascading over her body. The single photo and bland bio in her file hadn't done her justice. Beth was beautiful, stubborn, witty and intriguingly prim. A beautiful woman in mortal peril, he'd said to Jared. The phrase 'be careful what you wish for' hovered with taunting clarity in his mind.

Simon scrubbed his hands over his face as the water stopped, pushing aside thoughts of her wrapped in a towel, rubbing moisture from that luxurious mane of copper curls. He plucked the file from the bedside table and re-read the police report for the umpteenth time.

Burglars, the police concluded, taking advantage of a fault in the security gate which gave them easy access to the premises. Probably adolescents assuming a lab would hold drug-making equipment or a stock of pills. Finding nothing, they set a fire out of spite and left. The youths had not known anyone was inside.

Simon saw a few flaws in that argument. Beth's car had been parked directly outside, the only vehicle in the vicinity at that time of night, and yet the burglars hadn't assumed it meant someone was in the lab and they hadn't bothered trying to steal it.

These same alleged thieves hadn't just set one fire. They'd set numerous fires and all of them blocking the exit doors.

It didn't sound like juvenile drug seekers to him.

Simon went back to Jared's dossier, searching for another explanation. A crime of passion, a jealous wife? A love affair with a colleague? Stranger things happened all the time. However, Jared's comprehensive research had thrown up no significant relationships in Beth's life, failed or otherwise. His red-headed scientist was too involved in her work for social endeavours.

He grabbed his phone. Despite the early hour, Jared answered on the first ring. 'Problem?'

'Why is that always your first assumption?'

'I know you.' A hint of amusement coloured Jared's calm tone.

'Did we ever find out the exact nature of Beth's research project with Haden?'

'We did not. Haden Corporation said the information wasn't necessary for the assignment.'

'If it pertains to the nature of the fire, it feels necessary to me.'

'You're not investigating the fire, Simon, your job is to keep Dr Barrett safe, nothing more.'

Simon scanned the police report one more time. 'Fine.'

'Are you paying attention to a word I say?'

'I said fine. Kiss your beautiful wife for me.' Simon hung up before Jared could protest.

Leaving the file and the lumpy sofa bed behind, Simon strode to the kitchen, hoping food would take his mind off the beautiful woman under his care and the mystery surrounding her.

'You don't have to cook every meal for me,' she said minutes later, brushing past him to head for the kettle.

'I enjoy it. It's the most important meal of the day, remember.'

'I know. I always eat big in the morning in case I forget lunch.'

'I promise while I'm here, you'll eat regular meals.'

'Are we adding bossy to your character traits?' She turned from the counter to smile over her shoulder. Desire curled in Simon's stomach, and it wasn't for the food. Wearing an oversized tracksuit, her face scrubbed of makeup and her red curly hair gathered in a messy ponytail, Simon had never seen anything sexier.

Behave. You have a job to do. Remember, Jared will have your hide.

'Did you say something?' she asked.

'Nothing. Point me to your breakfast glasses. I'll pour the juice.'

They'd barely finished eating when the doorbell rang. Beth glanced up, frowning, and stood. Simon beckoned her back down, answering it himself.

Taking the flat box from the courier, he presented it to her.

Beth gave it a wary look. 'Don't you want to check it, in case it's a bomb or something?'

It dawned on him that she wasn't joking. 'The package is safe, I promise. I ordered it last night while you were sleeping, and had it sent by overnight express.'

She pulled off the lid with its discreet couture logo on the front, rummaged through a sea of tissue paper and pulled out a handful of soft, deep turquoise silk.

'For tonight,' he told her.

'Tonight?'

'The awards dinner. You said you had nothing to wear.'

'I didn't say that.' She stared at the pool of shimmering material in her hands. 'Where's the rest of it?'

Simon bit back a grin. 'This is directly from the Paris catwalks.'

'I think someone left half of it there.'

'It's beautiful. You'll look stunning in it. Trust me, I have a good eye. This is a special occasion. It requires a special dress. Why don't you try it on?'

'Now?'

'What's wrong with now?'

'Isn't it a bit fancy for this early in the morning?'

Simon couldn't help himself. He burst out laughing. 'Red, you're adorable. Early in the morning is the best time for fancy. Okay, I'll wait until tonight if I must.' He plucked the silk from her fingers. 'In the meantime, I'll hang it in the bathroom while I shower. The steam will smooth out the creases.'

She'd retrieved the mysterious box while he was away. Curiosity got the better of him, and he took a seat beside her as she ran her fingers over the stained cardboard.

'I can't believe my lab is gone.'

Simon placed his hand over hers for the briefest moment, enjoying the momentary contact. 'It isn't gone, just damaged. Is there anything you want to do today? Go for a walk? Watch TV?'

'Haden Corp texted. They're sending over some work.'

'I assumed you were on sick leave.'

'I need to work. I can't just sit here and do nothing. I'll go insane.'

He could relate to that. 'Okay, here's the deal. You work, I'll answer the door. Promise me?'

'You have my word.' She removed a manila folder, a box of glass slides, a portable hard drive and a microscope from the box. Simon reached out to touch the instrument. She scowled at him and he retreated, raising both hands in surrender.

Beth ran her fingers over the grey metal. 'Sorry. I've had this since my university days. It cost me every penny I had, and then some. I know it's old and outdated, but it's still my instrument of choice.' She nibbled on her lip, an action that caused Simon's stomach muscles to tighten. 'You may have noticed. I'm a little overly sensitive when people question my methods, *and* my age, *and* my qualifications.'

Simon couldn't help himself. He lifted her hand and pressed a kiss to her knuckles. 'Then consider me suitably chastised, Dr Barrett.'

'Are we—' she paused, and her throat muscles quivered as she swallowed, '—are we adding touchy-feely to that growing list of character traits?'

'Yes. I come from a large, gregarious family. Being tactile is in my nature. Slap me if I cross a line.'

'What? No, I ... it's okay, no slap required.' She tugged her fingers free and fiddled with the levers on the microscope, but not before Simon caught the blush of pink staining her pale cheeks.

'Is this part of your research?' He pointed to the glass slides.

'Yes. Double-blind tests from the past two weeks. At least it's a starting point for me to work on until Haden sends me more.'

'I'll leave you to work in peace.' Despite his ever-growing curiosity regarding the exact nature of her job, her pale skin and trembling voice spoke volumes about the residual emotions from her ordeal running just below the surface. As his *first* instinct of pulling her into his arms for a comforting hug didn't form part of his official duties, he went with instinct two, nourishing her with food.

His menu planning and cupboard rummaging were interrupted just minutes later by a mumbled curse. 'No, no, *no*. Dammit. I knew, I just *knew*.'

'What is it?'

'It's broken.' Her voice hitched on the last word as she cradled the microscope in her hands like a child. 'I heard a crack, and I hoped it was nothing.'

'I'm sorry.' That instinctive need to comfort her rose again, layered with a healthy dose of guilt. He put both hands on her shoulders. 'Did I cause it outside the hospital when I grabbed you?'

Sunlight shimmered in her bright hair as she shook her head. 'It was the fire's fault, not yours. It's all because of that stupid, pointless fire. I was careless and panicking trying to take the important stuff. The flames were everywhere. I couldn't focus.' The last words were bitten off with effort. She shook off his hands and stood, pacing the room, tension written into her every movement.

'What can I do?'

'Nothing.'

God, he'd never felt so helpless. A second ring of the doorbell broke the tense mood. Simon answered it, signing for the thick envelope marked *Haden Corp.*

Beth tore it open, some of the colour returning to her cheeks. Her expression fell when she examined the contents more closely. 'It's just paperwork.'

Her disgruntled tone made him smile. 'I take it you were expecting something a little more exciting?'

'This isn't even what I've been working on. It's routine stuff, invoices and book-keeping. I *hate* book-keeping.'

'Finally, a character trait we both share.'

She didn't respond, instead she spread out the folders on the dining table and picked up a pen.

As soon as she started working, Simon was forgotten. He grasped this after a short time and shook his head in rueful realisation. If he ever needed a woman to burst his ego balloon, this sexy scientist was the one to do it.

Chapter 2

Beth clipped together another pile of invoices relating to office stationery and kitchen expenses and signed her name to the appropriate spreadsheet. Returning the mind-numbing paperwork to its envelope, she gave her microscope a sad look. That ominous crack she'd heard during the fire had been the instrument's primary lens, the *one* thing a microscope couldn't do without. Although the back-up instrument she kept at home would do the job in a pinch, it didn't provide a fraction of the clarity and magnification she needed to keep her test result readings consistent. With a frustrated sigh, she packed the instrument away in a sturdier box and added her samples and hard drive. At least her slides weren't organic; they'd remain viable until she could resume her research. Beth couldn't say exactly *why* she hadn't told Haden Corporation about the items saved from the fire. She didn't consider the small omission a lie. From a professional point of view, she simply liked to double and triple check her own work and keep ahead of the curve.

Simon, true to his word, had left her in peace throughout the day. He seemed happy wandering around her house, cooking copious amounts of delicious food and even reading a racy romance book he pulled from her bookshelf. It was distracting seeing him sprawled in her favourite leather chair, legs propped up on her coffee table. As always, he was dressed immaculately in a blue shirt that matched his eyes and black trousers. The book cover currently in his hands was of a blond, muscled man wearing only a loincloth. Beth remembered the story being about some sexy barbarian hero who'd thrown the heroine over his shoulder and—

'Something wrong?'

'What? No? Why?' Beth stared at him without blushing only through sheer force of will.

'You had a funny look on your face.'

'No, no, it's fine, fine, all good, just working.' She gestured with the pen in her hand, almost poking her eye out in the process.

He put the book aside, shoving a paper marker in between the well-read pages to keep his place. 'You've been working too long. Time to stretch your legs.'

'In a minute.'

Beth squeaked as she found herself lifted from the chair with Simon's hands on her waist. 'Time to stretch your legs, madam scientist. Go for a walk around the room, look out of the window.'

Beth wagged a finger at him. 'You're impossible.'

'I know, Cec tells me all the time.'

'Cec?'

'Cecilia.' Another push, this one at the small of her back. 'Go on, walk. I'll bring you a coffee.'

Beth strode around the house a couple of times to stretch out her spine and shake the tension from her shoulders. She paused at her bedroom window and spied a utility truck and workers along the road. Was someone else in the street doing renovations? Good luck to them. Beth shuddered as she remembered the duel nightmares of government planning departments and Victorian plumbing she'd had to deal with, trying to make the rundown cottage into a livable home.

Simon pushed a cup of coffee into her hands. 'You should call it a day. It's almost time to get ready.'

'So soon?' Beth stared at her watch.

'It's past five. You don't want to be late for the ceremony.'

'Do we *really* have to go?'

'Yes, my little reluctant celebrity, we *really* have to go. What's the award for again? Apart from mould?'

'A young achiever's award for a scientific research paper on the positive properties of bacteria.'

He brushed a wayward curl away from her cheek. 'See? It's special. Okay, it's gross, but special. Go and get ready. I'll even let you have the bathroom first. That's how much of a gentleman I am.'

Why does the simplest touch of his fingers always linger so much on my skin?

After putting on her usual light application of make-up, Beth retreated to her bedroom and held up the turquoise dress in front of the mirror with a wary eye. Designed with a halter neck, the front and back of the dress both appeared to be alarmingly low cut. Layers and layers of translucent silk made up the bottom half. Leaving the designer garment on the bed, she picked out two pairs of shoes and studied them both. *Which ones would look better?* Beth had no idea.

Hearing a sound from the hall, she opened the door. 'Simon, what do you think—?'

The words died on her lips as broad shoulders and muscular arms filled her vision. Droplets of water dripped from the blond curls on his head and the sprinkling of matching curls spread across his chest, and that was just the *top* part of him. The towel draped over his hips did little to conceal the divine specimen of gorgeous almost-naked male standing in front of her.

'Sitting?'

Beth yanked her brain back into focus. He was talking to her. 'You want me to sit?'

Simon waved the shoes in front of her face, having plucked them from her fingers without her even noticing. 'I asked if we would be sitting. Isn't it a cocktail party? Or are we sitting for dinner?'

'Cocktail party, I think. Is that important?'

'These—' he held up the high heeled strappy black sandals, 'are sitting shoes. These—' he jiggled the mid-heeled silver-grey plainer ones, 'are standing shoes. How much do you want your feet to ache?'

'Not at all, preferably.'

'Good choice. Wear the grey. The dress has silver highlights. It will blend.' With that, he handed the two items back to her and continued along the corridor. Beth tried not to notice how the towel sat low across his back, just above muscular buttocks. *I need bigger towels.* A discreet cough made her gaze fly upward to meet his amused grin as he peeked over his shoulder.

'Are you staring at my backside, Dr Barrett?'

'Of course not.' Her denial was too loud, too husky. With yet another stain of heat burning her cheeks, she ducked back into her bedroom and wrenched the door closed.

Putting aside her misgivings about how small the dress looked on the hanger, Beth stepped into it, gaping at her reflection in disbelief. The couture garment fit perfectly. Falling in soft waves, it outlined her bust without clinging and fell to her knees in a shimmering kaleidoscope of turquoise. The color made her eyes appear extra green and her hair glow. Her skin had never looked so pale and perfect. She shook her head in wry amusement. Simon was right, damn him, he did have a good eye.

The next shock to her system came as she stepped out of her bedroom door and was confronted by Simon in a classic black tuxedo. Her steps faltered as brain and body momentarily misplaced the necessary physical actions required by walking. Simon looked great in regular shirt and slacks. In a tuxedo, he was devastating.

'Beautiful.' The word was a mere hum of sound on his lips. Crossing to her, he reached up, and with a single tug, undid half an hour of hard work on her hair. Released from its neat topknot, it tumbled down, sweeping along her bare back and making it clear just how much skin was exposed by the dress's halter neckline. The shock of it clicked her brain back into focus. 'Simon, that took me ages.'

'Oops, I'm contrite beyond belief. What a shame we've run out of time to fix it.' He ran his fingers through the riotous curls, setting them around her shoulders.

Beth could only chuckle at his reprehensible behavior and the innocent look on his face. He was impossible and cheeky, and gorgeous.

He held out his arm for her to take. 'Dr Barrett, your chariot waits.'

Once they were underway, he put music on, soft bluesy jazz that flowed out of the stereo. 'The work you were doing today. You said it wasn't your normal job, correct?'

'Correct.'

'Can you tell me what your normal research is?'

'Not really. They made me sign all sorts of non-disclosure contracts.'

'Let me guess. It's something to do with mould.'

Beth grinned at his teasing expression. 'Not this time.'

'It isn't a weapon, is it?' His tone dropped to a dramatic whisper.

The grin turned into genuine laughter. 'Nothing that exciting. The paper on mould you're *so* obsessed with brought me to the attention of Haden Corporation. They hired me to do research. That's all I can tell you.'

Simon flashed her one of his trademark grins. 'My sexy, secret scientist.'

Beth's blush started at the top of her head and didn't stop until it reached her toes.

People were gathering outside the exclusive London hotel. Beth recognised some familiar faces before Simon drove straight past.

'Simon, you've missed it.' Beth twisted in her seat, looking back at the disappearing building.

'No I didn't.' He pulled the car into the underground parking area of a large chain hotel down the street. A smartly dressed valet approached. Simon handed him the keys and pressed something into his hand.

'I don't understand.' Beth shook out her layered silk skirts as she alighted from the car. 'Why are we not parking at the function?'

'Because that's what people would expect. I don't like to be predictable. It's safer not to be.'

Beth bit back a giggle as she took the arm he offered. 'Why do I get the feeling you're *never* predictable?'

'Still alive, aren't I?'

'I'd say that's more about luck than your good judgment.'

Simon's expression was classic. 'Ouch, Red, you know me one day, and you already sound like Cec.'

Beth wanted to ask about this mysterious Cecilia that Simon spoke of so fondly. She held her tongue. Simon deserved his privacy too.

Tucking her arm in his, they strolled out of the lift into the crowded lobby. 'See, this is good, much more inconspicuous.'

Beth stifled more laughter with effort. Every single female and most of the men had turned to watch the elegant, tall tuxedo-clad man walk through the foyer.

'I hesitate to mention this, Simon. You're *not* an inconspicuous person.'

Waving his hand airily, he dismissed her wry observation.

Once inside the function centre, Beth scanned the flowing mass of people, most of whom she knew. She turned to Simon. 'Who are you going to say you are? You can't say bodyguard.'

'Don't worry, Red, I'll think of something.'

Haden Corp, for some reason she couldn't fathom, had made it clear her protection was to be done discreetly. *In which case, I shouldn't have brought Simon here tonight.* The circular logic of her current situation made her head spin. She snagged a glass of champagne from a passing waiter and groaned as she saw a figure moving in their direction. 'Damn.'

'What?'

'Pete Weaver, he went to university with me. We dated, *very* briefly, an unfortunate error on my part he likes to bring up every time we meet.'

Pete lived up to his surname, making his way through the crowds until he reached them, his gaze flicking over Simon before coming to rest on her. Beth had an urge to yank the couture dress up at the neckline.

'Beth, you look hot, as always.'

'Thank you.'

'And you are?' Pete turned to the man beside her.

Simon held out a hand. 'Dr Simon Winters, Professor of Archaeology at the University of Egypt.'

Beth choked on her champagne, clamping her hand over her mouth to catch the embarrassing spray of liquid. Simon pounded her on the back. 'Are you all right, darling? If you will excuse us, I think she needs some air.'

'What are you doing?' Beth poked him in the chest, trying not to grin as they took refuge behind a large pot plant on the balcony. 'If you're going to lie, at least make it convincing.'

Simon's expression was a captivating mixture of innocence and mischief. 'It seemed perfectly plausible to me.'

'Have you even been to Egypt?'

'Several times. I love the pyramids and films about mummies.'

Beth resisted the impulse to roll her eyes. 'Keep it simple, please. Don't load me up with a convoluted cover story I have to remember.'

'You're spoiling all my fun, Red.'

When they returned to the room, Beth gestured to three women waving at her. 'The other award nominees in my category. They insisted on coming along tonight, to congratulate me on my win.'

'Good for them.'

'They're nice. A bit more adventurous than me.'

'Good for them.'

The women made a beeline straight for them. They perused her date with intense interest and asked questions about the laboratory.

'Oh god, Beth I was away. I only heard this morning. Are you sure you should be here?'

'I'm fine, Madison, honestly.'

'But it was a fire, Beth, *a fire.*'

'Please don't be so dramatic. Do I seem horribly injured?' A tremor slid along her spine at the reminder of flames and smoke.

Simon's hand came down on her lower back to skim lightly over her skin. 'She's a lucky lady. Let's talk about something else, shall we?'

The trio of women nodded in unison. For the second time in minutes, Beth almost rolled her eyes. When was the last time a female had denied him anything?

Gwen, a sales rep, appraised him with unashamed interest. 'I'm sorry, have we met?'

His answering smile was polite. 'I don't believe so.'

Chloe put a hand on his arm. 'Are you sure we haven't? You look so familiar.'

Beth, not a violent person, had the unexpected urge to stamp on Chloe's designer-shod feet.

'I've been overseas recently, so, no, I don't believe any of our paths have crossed.'

Madison, another research analyst, was less subtle in her questions. 'Beth never mentioned you, Mr...?'

'Winters, Simon Winters. Beth and I only met recently. You could say I swept her off her feet.'

The three women sighed. Beth did another internal eye roll, which turned into a squeak when Simon tickled her side. Damn, this dress had way too many gaps in the fabric.

'We have to circulate,' he told the women in a courteous tone. Beth was certain only she heard the hint of amusement in it.

'Stop that,' she hissed at him as they turned away.

The blue gaze held only innocence. 'What?'

'You are never picking out my wardrobe again.'

'I'm staking a claim for the sake of appearances. You're so beautiful, all the men here are wishing they could take my place.'

'Don't be ridiculous.'

'I never lie.'

Alan Haden made his way through the crowded room waving in their direction. Beth lowered her voice. 'The CEO of Haden Corp is coming over.'

'I know who he is, Red.'

'Right, he hired you. I guess you've met.'

'Not in person.'

Haden reached out to touch her arm, dipping his head to be heard above the growing crowd noise. 'How are you, Beth? Should you even be here tonight?'

'I'm quite well, Mr Haden, thank you.' Beth tried to pull back, mainly to escape his cloying aftershave.

'I'm so terribly sorry I didn't see you in the hospital. I only returned from New York this afternoon. Did you get the flowers?'

'I did, they were beautiful.'

'Such a dreadful business to have all your research lost. Dreadful.'

'Not everything's lost.' The words were out of her mouth before she could stop them.

Haden's bushy brows rose skyward. 'Really?'

'I ... I just meant, I had some hand-written notes on my desk. I grabbed them before the smoke got too bad.'

'I see, I see. That's excellent news, my dear. As for the rest, we'll start again, better than ever, right? We should get together in my office in a couple of days and you can let me know how things are going. No rush. We all want you to recover fully from your traumatic experience. Ring my secretary and make an appointment.'

'I will, thank you.'

Haden turned his attention to Simon. 'You must be—'

'I am.'

'You're not what I imagined.'

'I'll take that as a compliment.' Simon's words were as cool and elegant as the neat bow that accompanied them. 'If you'll excuse us, Beth needs to be ready for the awards ceremony.' Nodding to her employer, he moved them away.

'You didn't tell him about your box of treasures.' Simon kept his voice low.

'Is that weird?'

'Depends. Are you breaching your contract?'

'No, it was more of a gut instinct.'

'In that case, go with it, Red. They always work for me.'

Gwen and Madison were gesturing from their position near the podium. Gwen, in particular, seemed more than eager to have Simon stand with them.

'Your fans are waiting.'

Simon grinned at her quip. '*Your* award is waiting. Let's go and get it.'

As one of the last awards of the night, Beth ended up doing a lot of standing around. *Thank goodness I wore the 'standing shoes'.* The thought resonated as she finally made her way up the steps to the stage without falling flat on her face. Simon cheered and clapped, encouraging everyone else to do the same. Beth tried giving him a threatening glare from her elevated position, which he promptly ignored.

Her acceptance speech defined the word concise and she stepped down in relief, glad to hand the attention to the next award recipient.

'No trophy? You were robbed.' Simon tucked her winner's certificate into his inner jacket pocket as the champagne flowed around them and people came over to offer congratulations.

'I don't need a flashy bauble.'

'Flashy baubles make the world go round. I fear your education is sadly lacking.'

'He's right, you know.' Gwen jangled the large pendant hanging from her neck, wobbling on her sky-high heels and giving Simon an eyeful of her ample bosom at the same time.

Madison clutched her hand before she toppled forward. 'Time to get you home, Gwenny, before all those champagne cocktails really kick in.' With the last award handed out, people were beginning to gather their coats.

'Aww, c'mon, Mads, the night is young. What about you, Beth, Simon, feel like hitting the clubs?'

Beth screwed up her nose in answer, even though Gwen's champagne-soaked focus was centred directly on Simon. To her surprise, Simon decided for both of them.

'Maybe another time? Beth only got out of the hospital yesterday.'

They nodded in contrite unison and left them alone, with reluctance if Gwen's pleading gazes were anything to go by.

'I take it you didn't want to go clubbing?' Simon took her arm and made their way through the departing crowds to the hotel's entrance.

'Not unless I've had a personality transplant in the last five minutes.'

'Would you contemplate coffee as an alternative? I know of a place nearby, nice and quiet, with actual food instead of those shrunken peas on a rice cracker we got tonight.'

Beth was barely listening. Her attention was locked on two men standing across the street.

'Red, what is it?'

'It's odd. I was looking out of my window earlier at home and I saw some workers parked a few doors down. I could almost swear those are the same two men.'

Simon put his arm around her waist and moved her out of the light. 'Where?'

Beth gestured without pointing. 'Over by that bistro.'

The larger man nudged his companion. They both peered across to where Beth and Simon stood.

Simon pushed her farther into the shadows. 'Are you sure it's the same people?'

'Something about the smaller man is familiar. The way he's pulling on his ear. Today he was wearing a hat, but he made the same gesture, like a nervous habit.'

'Let's play it safe and get out of here.' Without giving her a moment to think, he grabbed her hand and started walking. Left with little alternative, Beth trotted after him, as his long legs ate up the pavement. The laneways of this part of London resembled a rabbit warren, old and narrow. People were everywhere, spilling out on the footpaths. The district was trendy and bustling as was usual for a Saturday night. Although the crowds and darkness worked to their advantage, every time they passed a streetlamp Beth knew it was lighting up her damn hair like a beacon.

Simon looked back, his expression intense. Beth followed his gaze and sucked in a shaky breath. The men had given up any pretence of stealth and were picking up speed, shouldering people out of the way to get to them. Beth caught the thumping and pounding beat of dance music coming from another laneway just as Simon spun them into it. A group of revellers barred their progress, laughing and talking on the footpath. Simon pulled her closer, using the mass of humanity for cover. A door halfway along was lit with neon signs, some sort of nightclub. The music was muted, clearly coming from inside.

'Are we going in there?' Beth's whispered question was lost in the noise of the crowd.

Instead of answering, he pushed her against the wall, lifted both hands to the side of her head and kissed her.

The unexpected embrace was a shock to her system. Simon pressed his body against her, ripping a gasp from her throat at the full body contact. He absorbed that tiny noise with his mouth. His lips were soft and warm, a sharp contrast to the cold bricks biting into the bare skin of her back. He changed angles and slanted his mouth across hers. A quiver ran through her body at the bold intimacy of the caress. Simon pressed closer to stop the unconscious movement. Other couples were loitering close by, their passion-filled moans making it obvious what was going on under cover of darkness. Despite the emotion-filled intensity of the moment, Beth's inbuilt logic kicked in. *We must look just like them.* It was the perfect cover. Simon's hands on her head were shielding her bright hair from view, the shadows disguising their features.

A burst of chatter and an increase in the music broke the spell as more people spilled out of the nightclub door. Simon lifted his head and scanned the alley, holding her still.

'Okay, I think we're clear.' He lifted his warm body from hers and seized her hand, pulling her along the uneven paving. Beth stumbled and he steadied her, joining their bodies together for a second time. 'Are you all right? We can't stop here. Time is of the essence. We need to get back to the car.'

She nodded. 'Yes ... yes. I'm sorry.'

He hailed a taxi on the overcrowded main street but it ignored him. His muttered curse made his frustrations clear. 'Stay close to that doorway. I need to make a call.' He was still watching the street, his focus absolute.

Beth hugged her arms, the chill night air adding to the quivering radiating through her body. He was so focused. Calm and serious. All traces of playful Simon were gone. This tall, cold man talking inaudibly into a phone was a stranger.

Simon hung up and hailed another cab. Miraculously this one stopped. The journey was mercifully short, a mere few streets. Simon paid the driver without a word, grasping her hand as they waited in the underground area for his car. He stood silent and distracted. Beth was shaking and longed to be home.

Turning to her, Simon let out a breath, visibly releasing some of his tension. 'Slap me.'

'What?'

'A knee to the groin is also warranted. I'd prefer if you left that part until we get home in case we need to run from any more bad guys.'

Beth's head was still spinning. 'Why would I slap you when you just saved my life?'

'Are you kidding? I didn't just cross a line, I ran over it with a tank. I had to think on my feet. Sorry if I scared you.' He tucked a wayward curl behind her ear. 'It was necessary and at the same time unforgiveable. If you want to slap me, have at it.'

Although she knew he'd been doing his job, nothing more, the confirmation was embarrassing. A heated blush scorched her cheeks. Beth twisted her fingers in the delicate turquoise silk, silly tears threatening to humiliate her even further.

'Hey, hey, don't do that.' He tugged her into his arms for the *third* time that night. 'I didn't realise my kisses were so bad.'

She gave in to a watery, strained giggle. 'They're not. I'm just sorry you were *forced* to kiss me.'

He stroked her bare back with the tips of his fingers, making her twitch as he touched a tender spot.

'What's wrong? Are you hurt?' He pulled away, leaving Beth bereft of his body heat.

'Those bricks were rough. This dress has no back.'

Swearing under his breath, he shrugged out of his jacket and draped it around her shoulders, pulling her back into his arms again. Now she was surrounded by his warmth, the subtle smell of his aftershave clinging to the cloth. Beth's jangled nerves began to unwind.

'I couldn't think of another alternative plan in the short time we had.'

'It's all right, no slap required and I don't want to knee you in the p-privates either.' Beth shifted from one foot to the other.

'Are your feet hurting?'

'I think I have a blister on my heel. Maybe these aren't standing shoes after all.'

'Standing, maybe. Running? Definitely not. I am so sorry, sweetheart.' Simon's arms tightened, and he ran his hand gently up and down her back. Beth breathed in the endearment as much as the heat and warmth radiating from him. 'Can I tell you something?'

Beth nodded, and he bent his head to whisper in her ear. 'I'm sorry your special evening got spoilt. You were the most beautiful woman in the room tonight, and not just because of the dress, and I was very proud to be your date tonight. I enjoyed kissing you too, but there's a problem.'

She lifted her head to peer into his eyes. 'What problem?'

'You're an incredibly desirable woman, and I'd love to do *way* more than kiss you. Unfortunately, Jared has a clear no seduction clause written into this assignment. Sorry if admitting my attraction to you is a shock. At least I'm being honest.'

The valet pulled the car alongside, and Simon settled her in the passenger's seat. With a grin and a wink at her stunned expression, he drove them home.

༨༠

The buzz of a vibrating phone woke Simon. He reached for it as a muscle spasm sent a line of pain down his back. *This damn sofa bed is going to be the death of me.*

The message let him know the street was clear. The same text had come at two-hourly intervals since their return, as Jared's people drove around the quiet suburb.

Beth was moving around in the kitchen. Judging by the sounds coming from across the hall throughout the night, she'd barely slept. He'd given her space, even when every atom of his being wanted to be by her side every moment, watching over her, keeping her safe.

The rich aroma of coffee drifted into the room and Simon breathed it in, imagining her standing by the machine, pale and quiet. Anger surged through his body, borne of a fierce protective need as he lay with his arms behind his head, thinking. Two incidents, both seemingly involving Beth, with no discernible proof for either of them. Yes, they were followed on a busy London street by two men who Beth thought looked familiar.

Or, they were targeted by two would-be muggers drawn to the thought of rich pickings by Beth's couture gown and his designer tux.

Proof. He needed proof, and even more than that, he needed answers. Simon leapt from the bed and strode to the kitchen. Beth yelped as he spun her around to face him. 'Talk to me.'

'About what?'

'Everything. Your work. Haden Corp. This mysterious research project.'

'I told you I can't. I signed papers.'

'I don't care. Start from the beginning. Leave nothing out. What it is it? Chemical weapons? A super virus?'

Her coffee-scented breath fanned his face as she sighed. 'Textiles.'

Of all the things he'd expected her to say, that wasn't even on his list. 'Textiles?'

'Super lightweight, super strong textiles.'

'You mean material? Fabric?'

'Not just any fabric. Think of safety equipment that never degrades, Simon. Think of harnesses that can carry an incredible amount of weight and are almost weightless themselves. Not to mention various medical uses that haven't been considered yet. I'm thinking of a lightweight second skin to cover burns, to help the healing without leaving behind scars. Who *knows* what other uses Haden will come up with?' Her voice was rising, a palpable excitement reflected in her eyes.

'You invented this?'

Her laughter was light and open, and a joy to hear, considering the shadows of fatigue under her eyes. 'Thank you for the compliment, but no. Haden Corporation invented it. I'm just testing it.'

'Testing it for what?'

'Strength and degradation in every possible situation. Heat and cold, repeated exposure to various chemicals. All sorts of tests. So far, it's passing with flying colors.'

'This is why the Haden Corporation hired you?'

'They heard about my research papers and said I was the perfect candidate. They liked my reputation for detailed analyses.'

Simon stared at a point above her head, thinking. 'Why would someone want to blow up a lab testing textile strength? And why would someone want you out of the way.'

'Honestly? I don't know.'

'What's on that hard drive you have hidden away in your bedroom?'

'Test results.'

'Show me.'

She ducked under his arm and returned with the paperback-sized hard drive, plugging it into the laptop. A spreadsheet opened, with figures and numbers in neat columns. 'See? Test results. I send off samples to labs around the country to test for various conditions. They send the samples back. I check for degradation and compile a report.'

'There's more, isn't there? The slide box? These other folders?'

Beth shifted in her chair. 'Do you want the truth? I got bored. I thought I'd be involved in the actual testing, and yes, I got to check and recheck the lab results using my scope, except it was only a confirmation, an audit. I had an idea. The samples came back in tiny squares, like this.' She held up a slide. Simon took it from her fingers and examined it. To him, it looked like a miniscule half-inch of cotton, nothing more. 'After I compile the results, the slides are archived. I figured, why not use them, send them to other labs for re-testing. Break down the material further, test each individual strand. That's what I started doing. To you, it's a tiny square, to me it's an entire *world*. I'm used to dealing in miniatures.'

'Does Haden know this?'

Beth shook her head. 'I didn't inform the company directly. The re-tests are not a breach of contract, just an extra layer I did for my own personal enjoyment. It would have to be done eventually anyway. If the textile is to be used for medical procedures, possibly even inside the human body, it would need to be tested on an almost molecular level before being approved. Yes, I was jumping the gun a bit. I can't see how Haden Corp would object.'

'They'd object if there was something they didn't want discovered. What does this stuff look like when it's normal sized?'

'The textiles come in a variety of forms. Some are elastic, some aren't. Some are lightweight, almost silken, some are more robust. The flexibility is what makes it so tantalising, the possibilities are endless.'

'You don't have any bigger samples?'

'I handed them back straight after my initial interview, at their insistence. Haden keeps it all under lock and key. This is their baby. You can understand why they're so protective.'

Dammit, they needed more than a box of slides and a spreadsheet if they were to solve this mystery. 'Red, honey, I have an idea.'

'What sort of idea?' The look she gave him was wary.

Simon leant in closer. 'Want to break into your lab with me?'

༄

'Simon, this is insane,' Beth's voice was a whisper, her breath visible in the chilly morning air.

'No, it's a perfectly logical answer to our current lack-of-knowledge problem.'

'But it's a crime scene. Let's think about those words, shall we? *A crime scene.*'

'It's your laboratory, Red. You're allowed to go in there.'

She looked dubious. 'I don't have my passkey to open the security gates. I left it behind during the fire.'

'Which brings us to our first question. How did our burglars get in?'

'You read the police report. The gate jammed that day in the open position. Some electrical fault.'

'Convenient.' Simon peered at the building and its surrounds through the car's windscreen. 'It looks older in real life. Couldn't Haden have come up with something more modern for you to work in?'

Beth visibly bristled at the insult to the red brick structure. 'It has character.'

'I'm sure it has termites too.'

'It used to be a factory.'

'Were the workers ever allowed to leave? That's an impressively tall barrier. The word "prison" springs to mind.' Simon exited the car and gave the metal electric gate a tug. 'It's not moving now.' He eyed the high fence on either side. 'Wait there. I'll be right back.'

'What do you mean, right back?' Beth's hissed question faded as he climbed up and over the metal fence, landing on the other side. The security booth was easily breached and it took mere minutes to work out the controls and trigger the gates. *So much for security.* The sound of whirring machinery split the silent night air. Beth gaped at him in disbelief as he hopped back over the fence, slid back behind the driver's seat and waited for the gates to slowly open. 'You're impossible.'

'You keep saying that. Where shall we park?'

She directed him to the back staff parking area, hidden in the darkness by the building's looming shadow. Simon grasped her hand and switched on the flashlight, ignoring the remains of the yellow police tape still crisscrossed at the entrance. Soot and grime had fogged up the windows, leaving the entire area dim and gloomy.

'What exactly are we looking for?' She peered around the dark interior with some trepidation.

'Why are you whispering?'

'Because it's a *crime scene*, Simon.'

'Honey, you watch too many TV shows.' He examined their surroundings. 'What if the fire was designed to destroy all research as well as dispose of you?'

Beth scowled. 'You have a cavalier attitude to my near-death experience.'

He squeezed her fingers. 'I promise you, I do not. We should look for evidence of information that's been removed, specific things taken. You know what to look for, go and find it.' He handed her a smaller flashlight from his pocket and gave her a subtle push at the base of her spine.

'I'm able to walk without you doing that, you know.'

'I like doing that.' He winked at her. 'Go find us some evidence, madam scientist.'

'We should head for the main filing cabinets.' She directed them upstairs to the second level, pausing at the door to a windowless room. 'This is interesting. I assumed the fire or the water had ruined everything. It doesn't look like the fire penetrated this far in.'

Simon eyed their surroundings. 'Everything looks pretty soaked to me.'

'The hoses soaked everything. The main sprinkler system didn't activate. I thought you read the report.'

'It was a big report.'

'There may be a chance after all. Hold that thought. I need to get to the archives.' She hurried off down the hallway.

Simon pointed the flashlight at the ceiling, finding the small metal disc that represented the internal fire sprinkler system. 'Why didn't the main sprinklers activate?'

'I don't know.' Her voice came from further along the corridor. 'Simon, this would be easier if you would bring the big light over here.'

'Give me two seconds.' Simon tracked the sprinkler system with his beam, back to a main box on a wall. The casing was unlocked and opened with ease. He shone the light on the mechanism inside. Simon was no expert, tech wizardry was Bryce's job, but most fire sprinkler systems worked on the same basic principle. Stop valves. Alarm valves. Pressure switches and flow switches. The various components had to be locked in the open position in order for water to flow. These ones weren't.

'Simon,' Beth called out, 'these cabinets are open, and they shouldn't be. I think some of the files are gone.'

'I'll be right there.' Simon's fingers clenched on the torch as he took a closer look at the mechanics in front of him. The red isolating valve was not only closed, the heat sensitive element looked wrong, much newer than the surrounding equipment, as if someone had replaced it recently. If they had, and if he was correct, someone wanted to stop the sprinklers from activating, guaranteeing Beth a fiery death inside if the firemen couldn't get to her in time. *This was no common burglary or vandalism.*

Reaching into his pocket, he removed his toolkit. Perhaps he could get a clue from the newer element about who installed it and where it came from.

He saw the flaw in his plan a moment too late, as the system override reacted to his intervention.

Beth's cry of outrage echoed around the building as the deluge of water gushed from the now activated sprinkler system.

Simon used up his vast repertoire of curse words, trying to deactivate the system and shove water out of his eyes at the same time, to no avail. He surrendered the task and bolted to Beth's side. 'We need to go.'

'You think?' Yep, she was angry.

He had no time to apologise because right at that moment another voice joined the fray, a shouted command from outside the building.

'Great, *now* security arrives. Red, sweetie,' he grabbed her hand and pulled her along the corridor as she tried to push her wet hair away from her face, 'you know you said this was a crime scene and we shouldn't be here?'

'Yes?'

'You were right.'

'What?' She skidded to a halt, dragging him with her. 'You mean I'm going to get arrested for breaking into my own laboratory?'

He grinned through the torrent of water. 'Not if I can help it. I do suggest running as a viable option.'

They raced down the corridor as fast as the wet tiled floor would allow, heading for the stairs until Simon spotted the guard's flashlight heading up it.

'Okay, different plan.' He pulled her in the other direction.

Trying to clear his vision, he squinted left and right. 'If this was a factory, it should follow a standard floor plan, there should be a ... yes, an outside fire escape. Quick, this way.'

'Simon,' Beth yanked on his hand, 'that thing hasn't been used in years. I don't think it's even safe.'

'I'm sure it's fine. They built these things to last.' He tried the door. *Locked*. He drew another small kit out of his back pocket and bent to examine it.

'Simon,' Beth hissed in his ear, 'I can hear voices.'

'Patience, sweetheart.' He turned his attention to the lock. 'Come on, baby, release for me. Come on, sugar.'

Beth's startled laugh had a hysterical edge. 'It sounds like you're trying to seduce a woman instead of unlocking a door.'

'Distinct similarities, in my opinion. There you go, my darling.' The lock gave way under his prompting and he hauled Beth through the door onto the rickety fire escape.

'Stay here. I'll go first and test it for stability.'

'Test it for stability? What happens if it isn't stable?'

'We're about to find out.'

He raced down the old, rusty ladder leading to the lower levels, praying he wouldn't come across another security guard at the bottom. He didn't. Holding up his arms, he called to Beth, 'Come on, it's safe.'

'Simon,' she whispered down to him, 'maybe if we just explain, maybe they will understand.'

'Trust me, Red.' He caught her hands to help her down the stairs. 'I've been in this situation before. They never understand.'

They were both now on level one, and Simon headed down to the ground floor. Once there, he jumped down and held his arms up again. 'One more ladder, honey, and we're home free.'

Beth started her way down. When her foot reached the second rung, the rusted step gave way. Her cry ripped through the air as she was left hanging by her hands.

'Red!' Simon positioned himself directly underneath her. 'Just let go. I'll catch you.'

'I *can't*.'

'Yes, you can, just let go. I promise I'll catch you, I promise. Take a deep breath and let go.'

She did and Simon snapped his arms around her as the impact pushed him backward. He grunted as he twisted his body, hitting the ground instead of her.

'Whoa, I'm glad that worked.'

'What?'

Before she could berate him further, he yanked her to her feet and sprinted for the car. His progress was faster and he ended up grabbing her around the waist, almost tossing her inside when he opened the door. For once

Simon didn't even spare a thought for what their soaking wet clothes would do to the fine-grained leather. He rammed the key in the ignition and the powerful car roared to life, speeding toward the gates, the *closing* gates.

'Will we make it?' The panic in Beth's voice rendered it breathless.

Simon judged the distance with a seasoned eye. 'Yeah, we'll make it, but bloody hell, I really liked this car.'

The side of the security gate made a horrendous screeching sound when it ruined the pristine paintwork of the black Lamborghini as they roared through the closing gates.

Once he was sure they were clear from any pursuers, Simon pulled into a side street and ran his fingers through his wet hair before sneaking a peek at his shivering companion. Wet ringlets framed her face; her shirt was soaked, and, he couldn't help noticing, highly transparent.

'Are you okay?'

Beth glared at him, opened her mouth and then closed it again. She folded her arms across her chest and her expression could only be described as mutinous. 'I need to speak to your boss, right now, Simon.'

'Okay, we can do that. You might want to change clothes first—'

'I said *right now*.'

Chapter 3

'I'm sorry. This is never going to work. He's insane, completely insane.' Beth clutched the soft cashmere shawl closer to her body. The shawl, together with a hand towel, had been handed to her by a gorgeous woman in an immaculate business suit as soon as they'd arrived at the central London office. Almost as if wet, bedraggled, agitated clients turned up on the company doorstep every day. Maybe they did. Nothing would surprise Beth anymore.

Jared Knight sat behind a glass and oak desk, his arms on the chair, hands casually clasped, as Beth paced back and forth across the spacious office. 'We truly feel Simon is the best man to protect you, Dr Barrett. After all, he hasn't managed to kill himself yet.'

'Yet!' She waved an accusing finger at the agency head. 'Haven't you noticed, he tries all the time, usually when he's standing right next to me.'

The object of her accusations, currently leaning nonchalantly against the wall with his long legs crossed at the ankle, put up his hand to be noticed as she strode past him. 'I'm right here.'

She whirled on him. 'Then I'm probably in danger.'

'Simon, would you like to speak in your defence?' Jared asked, in a voice that defined the word unruffled.

'The sprinkler system was tampered with.'

'Are you certain?'

Beth paused in her pacing to listen. 'You said yourself it's an old building. The gate broke down that day, maybe it was another electrical fault.'

'I know the difference between on and off, Red. No water, no sprinklers.'

Jared steepled his fingers. 'You have a theory?'

'Nothing that can be proven, not yet anyway. Beth said papers had been removed from cabinets, conveniently *not* soaked by water.'

'Dr Barrett?' Jared addressed the question to her.

Beth dragged a still damp curl out of her eye. 'I didn't have a chance to get specifics of what was missing. It was too dark and I was interrupted by an internal waterfall.' She threw Simon an accusing glare which he answered with a semi-apologetic grin.

Beth turned her attention to Jared. 'Mr Knight. Yes, I appreciate Mr Haden's concern for my welfare, but surely none of this has anything to do with me. I'm just the researcher. I like my life quiet, peaceful and orderly.

He,' she jabbed a finger in Simon's direction, 'wouldn't know what peaceful and orderly meant if it jumped off a high building and fell on him.'

'You do know I *can* hear you, right?' Simon raised both hands in surrender when she rounded on him.

'Are you in trouble again?' A low, melodious female voice sounded from the doorway.

Beth spun to see a woman standing there. An utterly beautiful, hugely pregnant woman dressed in a flowing maternity dress. Dark curly hair flowed over her shoulders, held back from her face by sunglasses perched on her head. She strolled into the office with graceful elegance despite her large stomach.

Simon let out a cry of pleasure and surprise, rushing toward her, meeting her in the middle of the room. He grabbed her, bending her backward over his arm in a dramatic dip. The woman's peal of laughter was filled with affection, if a little breathless. She grasped his shoulder with one hand to steady herself and grabbed her tummy with the other.

'My dark-haired beauty,' he muttered in a stage whisper loud enough to be heard in the next suburb, still holding her in the dramatic pose. 'My epitome of womanhood.'

Something in Beth's heart twisted. *Simon's married and about to be a father.*

She mentally berated herself. Why wouldn't he be married? He was gorgeous, clever and funny *and he'd kissed her*. Beth ignored the pang in her chest. He'd kissed her as part of his job.

Jared put both hands on his desk and stood. Striding across the room, he took the woman by the arm, pulling her from Simon's embrace into his own. She was still laughing, her face flushed. Jared snaked an arm around her midriff, his hand coming to rest with possession on her tummy.

The agency head threw a frown at Simon, who ignored it. 'Red,' Simon gestured to the couple, 'this beautiful creature is Cecilia, Jared's wife. And this,' he put his hand with casual familiarity next to Jared's on her extended tummy, 'is my godson.'

'Or goddaughter,' Cecilia corrected.

'Or goddaughter,' Simon echoed. 'If it's a boy, I'm going to take him skydiving on his sixteenth birthday.'

Cecilia Knight, *not* Cecilia Winters. 'What if it's a girl?' Beth asked, shoving aside the illogical bloom of happiness at the marital clarification.

A wrinkle formed between Simon's brows as he gave the matter some thought. 'If it's a girl, we'll still go skydiving, but she isn't allowed to date until she's thirty.'

Cecilia's chuckle echoed in the room. 'That one single point is about the *only* thing her father and godfather will agree on, the dating part anyway.' She patted Jared's hand. 'Could you give us a moment alone please?'

Jared tipped up his wife's face with his forefinger, planting a feather-light kiss on her mouth. Beth watched with another pang of envy at the laden emotion in that small gesture. He withdrew his arm from around her and headed toward Simon, who was talking at a rapid pace.

'Alone? You mean just the two of you?' he was still complaining as Jared, not even breaking his stride, caught him by the arm and propelled him from the room.

'Girls' talk, Simon,' he said as he closed the door behind them.

Beth had never been the most self-confident of people. Now, standing next to Cecilia Knight, disheveled and damp, she understood the very definition of awkward. To make it worse, Cecilia didn't speak, just watched her with a curious expression. To break the silence, she asked, 'When are you due, Mrs Knight?'

Cecilia smiled, her hands going to her tummy. 'Call me Cecilia, please. The official due date is two weeks. I know it looks like two minutes.' She sighed, eyeing her protruding stomach with a wry look. 'They keep assuring me there's only one in here. Personally, I won't be convinced until only *one* comes out. Jared tells me he was a tiny six pounds at birth. I think he's trying to ease my mind. I fear there's a nine-pounder in here for sure. How are you dealing with Simon?'

Beth was taken aback by the unexpected change in topic. 'Simon? Well, he's, I mean, he's—' Giving up on her stammering explanation, Beth flopped down in the visitor's chair. 'He's driving me crazy.'

Cecilia chuckled, then winced as the baby responded to her humour with an obvious kick. 'He's a character, isn't he? Don't let that playboy image fool you. A clever brain and a big heart lurk beneath that devil-may-care exterior. I assure you if I were in danger and Jared couldn't be with me, I know he'd want Simon there, and if you knew my husband, you'd realise that's a massive compliment. I won't bore you with the details, but if it weren't for Simon Winters, I possibly wouldn't be here today. Don't write him off just yet. Give him a chance.'

'Cecilia, he's so impulsive. He leaps in where angels fear to tread.' Beth pulled the shawl closer to her body, fiddling with the fringed edge.

'I'm not aware of the details of his assignment with you. I'm guessing it's connected to some form of personal danger?'

'That's the general consensus, although no one can figure out the important parts, like who, or why.'

Cecilia lowered herself into Jared's leather office chair, her expression turning serious. 'Do you know what an unknown threat is? It's a shadow in your peripheral vision. One that never goes away. Trust me, Beth, you don't want to live with that shadow, not for one second longer than you have to.'

'That's what the police investigation is for. They'll find the answers, that's their job isn't it?'

'They *might* find the answers. I'll tell you one thing for certain. Simon *will*. He'll solve the mystery. He'll flash that shadow out of existence even if he has to harness the sun to do it.'

Beth hesitated before speaking. 'He said he's attracted to me, but it's not really me. It's the danger, the thrill of the chase.'

'Do you know what Jared's team have in common? They're searching for something, all of them, even if they don't realise it. That's my opinion anyway. Jared raises his brows at me, but I stand by it. Simon is the worst offender. Always running, always seeking danger. It's a habit. They're all still living their old lives until something real and important comes along. Tame Simon, and you'll have the most wonderful man on your hands.'

Beth raised her hands in denial. 'Oh no. I mean, I don't want him on my hands, tame or otherwise, I assure you.'

Cecilia pointed to the glass office wall where they could see Jared leaning against a leather chair in the waiting room watching the two women talk and watching Simon pace.

'I'm going to share something with you. I've seen Simon with women before. He's the ultimate in cool, calm and collected. Tell me, does he look cool, calm and collected now?'

Beth snuck a peek at the men, as Simon ran both hands through his blond curls, destroying the trendy just-got-out-of-bed look. 'No.'

'That change, it means something. You mean something to him.'

'I'm sure that's not true.'

'Trust me on this one. Give him another chance.'

'What if all of this, this craziness turns out to be nothing. A coincidence? A wild goose chase? A storm in a teacup? What happens then?'

Cecilia's shrug was almost as elegant as one of Simon's. 'Then you'll go back to that calm, orderly life you cherish so much and have some interesting stories to tell in your old age.'

Beth wasn't aware she made a sound of compliance, but Cecilia smiled at her, gesturing to her husband.

Jared returned to his office and took up his former position next to his wife. Simon followed close behind, his expression an interesting mix of worried and hopeful.

'Well, Dr Barrett?' Jared asked. 'Do we find you another protector?'

Beth studied Cecilia, then Simon. 'I don't want an unknown threat hanging over my life. I need to solve this mystery. I've been reliably informed you're the person to do it. So, I'm giving you one more chance.'

Simon whooped and grabbed her around the waist, spinning her around and planting a kiss on her mouth. She pushed him away – well, tried to, as her feet were off the ground at the time. 'Stop that. Put me down, you idiot. I *will* slap you this time.'

'Have at it, Red. I just had to do it once.'

'Twice.'

'*Fine*, once without us being in danger.'

Jared made his way toward his office door with Cecilia by his side. 'Please try to remember, Simon. The object of the assignment is to save Dr Barrett from perilous situations, not create them.'

Simon released her and pointed a finger at Jared. 'It isn't as bad as she makes it sound.'

Jared looked skeptical. 'My wife and I have a doctor's appointment. We will see you later.' He inclined his head to Beth. 'Dr Barrett.'

'A pleasure to meet you,' Cecilia added, and then to Simon, 'Be good.'

'I'm always good.' Simon's grin sent an odd shiver of anticipation down Beth's spine.

I'm probably making the biggest mistake of my life. Is it crazy that at this moment, I don't care?

Beth tapped the edge of the pen against her mouth. A lined pad rested on her drawn-up knees as she sat sideways on the sofa. 'What do we know?'

Simon handed her a cup of coffee. He peered at the pad, his proximity affording her a tantalising whiff of his lemony aftershave. 'Judging from that blank page, not much.' He ran his fingers over the back of her neck and trailed them through her ponytail. 'Do you make lists of everything?'

Beth flicked her hair over her shoulder, dislodging his questing fingers. She ignored the flicker of sensation his touch caused on her bare neck. 'It makes sense to make lists, that way nothing gets missed. Don't you make lists?' A wide smile met her enquiring look. 'What am I thinking? Of course you don't.'

'What do we know?' Simon repeated her question.

'We possibly know that you think Haden Corporation is trying to hide something.'

'It makes sense. It's likely they assumed you were only using their laboratories. Therefore, they could control the test results coming back to you. Your use of independent labs and more in-depth testing takes that control away. Something spooked them. We have to find out what.'

'What could spook them enough to take such drastic action?' For a moment Beth was confronted by a memory of flames and burning hot air in her lungs.

Simon touched her bare neck again, this time his fingers moving in a circular massage, relieving her tension. She dipped her head, giving him permission to continue, amazed by his perception of her moods. She wrote the words *independent laboratories* on the pad and underlined them.

Simon moved to sit down beside her. He tugged at her drawn-up legs, pulling them across his lap. He was so naturally tactile. *I could get used to this.*

'How many test results are you waiting for?' he asked.

'Dozens.'

'What's to say the laboratories themselves are not in danger?'

'It's all blind testing. Totally anonymous. There's no list of labs receiving the samples, not by name anyway, just code numbers. The labs themselves work on the same system. All the samples are number coded. The results are sent back to a post office box. It's the way I always do things, total anonymity. I've worked with most of the labs before, and the number system prevents any personal preference of mine regarding their methods influencing the results.'

His smile was enough to send butterflies to her stomach. 'My wonderful, brilliant little scientist. What about the post office box? Could Haden try to steal the results from there?'

'It isn't in my name, and it's in the city. It gets checked daily and I get a message in a separate email account, one I don't use for anything else, to say when there's something to be collected.'

'Clean, simple, methodical, organised. That's very you, Dr Barrett.'

Beth sniffed at his teasing tone and pulled her legs from his lap.

He leaped up from the sofa, startling her, and bent to place a kiss on the top of her head. 'Can you check? Do we need to go and collect samples today?'

'If there are some waiting, I'll arrange a courier.'

'If we collect them ourselves, we may lure out anyone trying to find out more information.'

'Absolutely not, Simon.' Beth scrambled to a kneeling position. 'This system works perfectly well in its current format, and the last thing I want is to lose more data. Or place other laboratories in danger. A courier can bring the samples back here, and I can analyse them and try to work out what Haden is trying to hide, or if you're really paranoid, we can have two couriers, changing hands at some neutral location, like a second post office.'

'Arrange the neutral location. I'll get Two-Jay to pick up the samples and bring them here.'

'Who?'

'Jared's PA. You met her at the office.'

'What's her real name?'

'How do you know it isn't Two-Jay?'

'Because I'm getting to know *you*.'

'Her name's Jade. Jared and Jade? That's *way* too confusing, not to mention sounding like a bad sitcom. So she became Two-Jay.'

'Because she's the second J.'

'You've cracked it. I started out calling Jared Two-Jay instead. He threatened to shoot me. He does that a lot.'

'Cec and Two-Jay. Do you ever call anyone by their actual name?'

'Of course I do ... Red.' That megawatt smile sent her tummy into its usual flip-flop manoeuvre. 'How are you going to do the testing? Your microscope is broken.'

'I have a spare.'

'Of course you do. Are you always this annoyingly logical and organised.'

'I like being logical and organised, I like being methodical. I like to take my time, do things properly and get satisfactory results.'

He sauntered toward her like a large, lazy cat and stopped with his face close to hers. 'So do I. Satisfactory results are immensely enjoyable.'

Simon was going to kiss her again. *That's a bad idea. It's totally a bad idea.*

He winked instead and spun on his heel, heading back toward the kitchen. 'You ring the courier. I'll ring the office.'

He was being professional. She told herself she was relieved. At no point did she believe it.

She was less relieved and more frustrated the following morning when things did not go to plan. The long-awaited samples arrived late in the evening. Beth had worked into the night, even after Simon went to bed, and the results had *not* been satisfactory. She had to face facts. The secondary microscope was a backup, a less powerful instrument and not up to the task.

A knock sounded at her bedroom door. Simon's voice was muffled through the barrier. 'Hey, sleepyhead, are you okay?'

'Yes.'

'Can I come in?'

Beth scrutinised her outfit. The tracksuit was old and covered everything. 'All right.'

Simon shouldered open the door and strode in. His fair hair was darker for being wet. He was bare-chested and wore only a pair of casual tan-coloured trousers. *Well, that's certainly a distraction.* In his hand he carried a complex breakfast tray, which he lowered to her lap.

'You didn't have to make me breakfast.'

'Of course I did. If Dr Barrett will not come to food, it will have to come to her. Penny for your thoughts?' He gestured to the bed, asking for permission, and she nodded.

'Are we overreacting?' she asked.

'About what?'

'Everything.'

Simon sat and swung his legs over to lie beside her, leaning against the padded headboard, stretching out his long legs and crossing his ankles.

She had to smile. 'Do you practise that?'

'What?'

'The *Simon Sprawl.*'

The comment earned her a lazy grin. 'I do recall school reports complaining about my feet on desks, and my mother has the occasional grumble about scuff marks on her coffee table.'

Beth could imagine him as a teenager in high school, unruly blond hair, females falling at the altar of his burgeoning beauty.

Rolling to one side, Simon reached out and snagged a piece of diced melon from a bowl. 'It isn't an overreaction. Those men chased us through the streets, the same men who'd been hanging around *your* street.'

Beth rolled the warm mug of tea between her palms. 'Maybe I was wrong. I didn't get a good look at them.'

Lifting the fork from the tray, Simon speared a piece of pineapple and held it to her lips. 'Eat.'

Beth pulled the succulent fruit from the tines with her teeth. 'But, Simon …'

'Eat first, talk later.' He tapped her nose with the fork.

She frowned at him. 'As a scientist, I can tell you that utensil is now contaminated.'

Simon put the fork in his mouth and returned it to the tray. 'All better.'

She had to smile. 'No, it isn't. Now it's even more contaminated.'

'I have to say, Red, having a romantic breakfast with you is challenging.'

'Is that what we are doing? Having a romantic breakfast?'

'Absolutely not. I am under strict instructions not to flirt or seduce you, remember?' Resting casually on one elbow, he was overwhelmingly male in her soft feminine bedroom.

'Do you have those orders for all your personal protection assignments with women?'

'I never get personal protection assignments with women. You're the charming exception.' He reached out a hand and tucked a curl behind her ear.

Beth raised her fingers to her head. 'I must look a fright.'

'You look beautiful, sleepy-eyed, and deliciously tousled.'

'Is this you *not* flirting?'

'Yes, how am I doing?'

'Dreadful.'

'Shall we try not seducing and see if that works better?'

Beth's breath caught in her throat, and her answer came out huskier than she intended. 'Do I need to ring your boss?'

Another lazy smile, and his eyes twinkled with mischief. 'I told you. Jared isn't really my boss, he simply does all the organising and paperwork the rest of us hate.' Simon reached over and took a piece of toast from the silver toast rack. Beth couldn't even remember *having* a silver toast rack.

'Jared met Cecilia when he was her protector, didn't he? So I guess he broke the no flirting rule.'

Simon's laugh was a seduction technique in its own right. 'I happen to know Jared spent most of the time standing a suitable distance away, wearing a serious, brooding expression and being very well behaved. He didn't even call her by her first name.'

Beth watched the handsome man sprawled half naked on her bed stealing food from her tray. 'I take it that isn't your style, *Mr Winters*?'

'No, *Dr Barrett*, that isn't my style at all.'

'Did you make this breakfast for you or me?'

'Both of us.' He stole another piece of toast.

'I suspect you're just trying to cheer me up.'

'I am. Want to tell me what's up this morning? I heard the odd curse word late in the night.'

Lifting the fruit bowl before he ate all of it, she sighed. 'I'm sorry if I woke you. All our careful planning was for nothing. I need my proper scope.'

'The broken one? What's wrong with it exactly?'

'The primary lens is damaged.'

'A glass lens?'

'Of course.'

'Why didn't you say so? I know someone who can help.'

'Simon, don't be ridiculous. These are specialist instruments. Even if I send it away, it won't come back for months. You cannot possibly know someone who can fix it.'

He grinned. 'You haven't met Jet. Eat up, Red, and get that gorgeous body into the shower. I'll call a taxi, then we're going out.'

'If you like old buildings, you'll love Bryce's place.'

'Simon, it's a converted Victorian warehouse right on the Thames, this place must be worth a fortune. What is it with you and historical buildings?'

'I grew up in an old house. I prefer modern now.' Simon inserted the key into the solid steel front door and shouldered it open.

'Are you sure this is all right? It's very early and you didn't even call him first.' Beth rubbed her hands to ward off the chill of the morning air.

Simon gave her a smile. 'I promise you, Jet's a night owl, and if anyone can help you, it's him. There's nothing he can't build and nothing he can't fix. Oh, and no lock he can't pick. He's handy to have around. Jet, are you here?' Simon yelled the question into the spacious entranceway.

An ominous tinkling sound came from their left. A sound very much like something small, delicate and expensive breaking.

Simon took her hand and pulled her into the room. A dark-haired man sat with his back to them, beside an antique looking desk. His shoulders had a tense look about them.

'Hi, Jet.'

The shoulders sagged and the figure turned to face them. He held a technical instrument in one hand and a small piece of broken equipment in the other.

Simon's expression turned sheepish. 'Sorry, was that my fault? If it's any consolation, we need your help.'

No response.

Simon pulled her in front of him like a shield. 'Forget about me. *She* needs your help.'

The man put down his work and stood, holding out his hand to her. 'Bryce Black. Let me guess, you were in trouble, and since meeting Sir Simon, you've had numerous near-death experiences and now you're in even more trouble?'

Beth shifted her box to one hip and shook the offered hand. 'That about sums it up. Why does Simon call you Jet?'

'Because he has an annoying habit of giving people nicknames. Have you noticed?'

Beth grinned at his raised brow look. 'I have.'

'I resent the numerous near-death experience comment.' Simon moved to one side and took up a stance against the wall. 'Anyway, Jet makes perfect sense. Bryce Jethro Black? Who saddles their son with names like that? Jet's easier, and it fits.'

'Jet Black? Like on a colour chart?' Beth threw Bryce a look of sympathy.

He winced and nodded. 'You?'

'Red.' Beth tugged at her hair.

'Ah, of course. Colour-coded nick-names are his favourite. You must be Dr Barrett. I saw your file come across Jared's desk. You're Simon's dream assignment. A beautiful woman in peril, wasn't that the requirement, Simon?'

Beth scowled at her protector with suspicion, before turning her attention back to the matter at hand. *That* particular morsel of information could wait until later. 'Call me Beth, please. No offence, Bryce, I know Simon said you could help, but if we're wasting your time, I'll understand.' She removed the scope from its sturdy box and handed it over.

His hum of approval put her mind at ease. 'This is a beautiful instrument, have you had it long?'

'Since my uni days. The main lens has a crack.'

Bryce put the instrument on the table. He selected numerous tools and painstakingly removed the glass under Beth's watchful eye. 'What are you using this for?'

When no one replied, Bryce looked up, glancing from her to Simon. Simon left his spot by the wall to put his hands on her shoulders. 'You can trust him, Red.'

Delving back into the box, she retrieved the slides. 'I'm analysing textile samples.'

'Thank you. I don't need the details. I just need to know how to configure the lens.'

Beth sat down to watch him work, and couldn't help comparing the two men. With dark hair and unusual amber-coloured eyes just visible through the tinted glasses he wore, Bryce was the polar opposite of Simon.

He interrupted her silent perusal. 'I can fix this for you. It may not be exactly the same as the original if you need me to do it quickly, but it will be almost the same magnification you're getting now.'

'Are you sure?'

'Absolutely.'

'Thank you.' Beth jumped up to hug him and press a kiss to his cheek.

'May I keep the slides?' She bit her lip and he added, 'It will enable me to know when I have the lens correctly set and will save time. I assure you, Dr Barrett, my house is perfectly secure. Your work will be safe here.'

Beth nodded her agreement. 'Is there anything I can do to help?'

'Nothing at all. Make yourself at home. No doubt Simon already has.' Bryce didn't look up from his work.

'What?' Simon asked in innocence when Beth turned to see him sprawled across Bryce's leather couch. With a shake of her head at his cheekiness, and with her naturally curious nature piqued, she began to explore. Bryce's home was a treasure trove of antique instruments, mixed with modern high tech equipment. She was drawn to one item in particular, a giant faceted diamond mounted on a delicate pewter stand.

'Is that real?' She addressed the question to Simon.

'Technically, no. It's one of Jet's creations. He makes great replica diamonds.'

'For goodness' sake, you say that in the same casual way someone would say, "oh, Jet makes great cheese sandwiches".'

'He doesn't make great cheese sandwiches. Mine are much better.'

Beth rolled her eyes. 'Bryce, this is incredible.'

'Thank you.' His voice was distracted as he had her scope partly disassembled. 'I like glass. I like the refraction and magnification qualities.'

'How do you even make replica diamonds?'

'Time, patience and methodical diligence,' he replied, throwing Simon a meaningful look.

Beth burst out laughing at Simon's offended expression. 'Yes, well, I have other talents.'

She gave up her exploring to watch Bryce work, fascinated by his obvious skill and expertise.

'Two days?' she said a few hours later. 'Are you sure that's all you need?'

'That will give you enough strength to do what you need, Dr Barrett. You can always bring it back later, and I'll do a proper job.'

'Thank you.' She hugged him again. 'And please, just call me Beth.'

Bryce inclined his head. 'Beth it is then.'

Simon stood and stretched. 'I guess we'll be back in two days. Jet, can I borrow your car?'

'After what you did to Lucien's? Certainly not.'

'I don't know why people have to bring that up. The lake wasn't that deep.'

Beth studied the two men. 'What happened?'

Simon waved his hand. 'A tiny altercation between a helicopter, a speeding train and a small body of water.'

'And a brand new Bentley straight out of the showroom. You do remember Luc refused to talk to you for three months after that and Jared was fuming.'

'Is it my fault Lucien suffers from mood swings and Jared has no sense of adventure?'

Bryce folded his arms. 'What about all your cars?'

'The Lambo is damaged and I don't have time to go home and get another one.'

Beth tapped him on the arm. 'I have a car. The police took it for fingerprinting after the fire. I gather they found nothing. There's no reason why we can't have it sent back to my house.'

'Why didn't you say something before?'

She scowled at him and planted her hands on her hips. 'You dragged me into a waiting taxi before I had a chance to say anything, as usual.'

Bryce chuckled. 'Is it a fast car? That was another one of Simon's dream job requirements. Careful, Beth, he'll fall in love with you if it is.'

A rush of anticipation set Beth's heart fluttering. 'I guess we'll have to see if it meets Simon's demanding approval.'

Chapter 4

'Beautiful, absolutely beautiful.' Simon ran his hands over the sleek surface of the vehicle.

Beth tapped her foot on the ground. He hadn't been this enthusiastic when she'd been standing in front of him wearing a backless couture gown.

'You have a Ferrari, a *red* Ferrari convertible. This is why your garage has such excellent security when your house was average. It all makes sense now.'

For some reason, Beth had an urge to justify her extravagance. 'It's second hand, not new, and it was an impulse buy after I got my advance from Haden Corp. I went in to get something roadworthy and sensible and got sidetracked.'

He shot her a grin. 'Everyone's entitled to one day of madness, even you. Admit it. You love it.'

'I do.' *Apparently not as much as Simon does.*

'Let's go for a drive.' He opened the car door and nudged her into the passenger's side.

'Where?'

'Anywhere.'

Her phone rang and she stopped scowling at her impulsive protector to answer it. 'Hello, Mr Haden, how are you?'

Simon gestured for her to put the phone on speaker.

'Excellent, thank you,' Haden said, 'I trust you're quite recovered?'

'Yes, thank you, did you still want me to come into the office?'

'I do, whenever you have time. To discuss your progress.'

Simon put the key in the ignition. Beth shook her head at him.

'I have meetings most of the day,' Haden continued, and Beth threw Simon a smug look. Simon pouted and removed the key.

'Perhaps later? At the end of the working day? Say around seven?'

'Perfect, we'll see you then.'

'We could go around the block?' Simon suggested with a hopeful glance her way when she hung up.

'Or you could go inside and cook that meal you promised me.'

'I can make pasta, if we had eggs.' His expression was openly pleading.

Beth surrendered the battle. 'Go to the shops, get it out of your system.'

'I can't leave you alone.'

'I'll lock the door, I promise, and huddle in the living room away from the windows. Just go. Do not crash my car and try not to drool on the upholstery.'

'You are a hard taskmaster, Dr Barrett.' Simon pecked her on the cheek before diving into the driver's seat. 'But you have fantastic taste in cars.'

After dinner, fresh pasta as promised, she stepped back into the garage, smoothing down her navy blue jersey dress. Had she changed into this for Mr Haden? Or for Simon? The man of her thoughts had removed the roof of the Ferrari and was bent over the door peering in the glove box, giving Beth a clear view of a muscular backside outlined in charcoal-gray trousers.

'What are you doing?'

He turned with a grin. 'Playing. Come on, the trip should take an hour using the back roads.' Opening the passenger's side door, she automatically got in at his urging and realised her mistake.

'Wait. This is my car. Why are you driving?' It was too late. He was pulling out of the garage.

'You can drive back.'

'Since when did my car become joint custody where we take turns?'

'It's a—' he paused, 'a security measure.'

'Is that why we're taking the back roads?'

'Of course.'

'Not because you want to act like a teenager?'

'Absolutely not.'

Ten minutes later, she suppressed another scream as he took the corner at breakneck speed. 'She's gorgeous,' he said, speaking loudly to combat the roar of the engine. In Simon's hands, the Ferrari came alive. As if knowing it had met an expert, the red beast purred and responded to his every move.

'Are you going to tell me again this is for security? And not because you want to play with my car.'

He turned his attention from the twisting country road. 'Do you doubt me, Red?'

'All the time. Let's get this straight right now. I'm driving home.'

'Naturally. It will be your turn.' He blew her a playful kiss.

Beth surrendered to her laughter. He was crazy, and for the foreseeable future, he was *her* crazy.

At ten minutes after seven, he pulled into the car park at Haden Corporation. Beth tried to tame her windblown hair. She hadn't had a chance to tie it back and the roofless car had created havoc with the curls.

'Beautiful.' Simon looked up from the dashboard and straight at her.

'Beautiful.' He repeated the word, running his hand down her madly cascading mass. The simple action sent her tummy flip-flopping.

He was a flirt. He flirted with women as naturally as breathing and it didn't mean anything. Beth couldn't convince herself this time that she was relieved.

Simon peered around the large compound. 'Is this place just offices? Or labs as well.'

'Both. Research and Development is over there.'

'I guessed that from the fence and gates. These people take their research seriously.'

'They're security conscious.'

'I'm still getting a prison vibe.'

Beth ignored the taunt. 'The far corner building is for simulations. This one here is admin and office personnel.' She pointed out the various wings.

'At least it's modern. You should be working here instead of that red brick death trap they had you in.'

Beth slapped him on the arm. 'Will you *stop* insulting my lab.'

He took the abuse with his usual grin. 'I'm just saying. You're the best. The best of the best. You deserve the head office, that's all.'

Damn it, if her organs kept flip-flopping like this, she'd end up on life support. 'Thank you.' Her apology was a garbled murmur as she willed the ever-present heat from her cheeks.

A secretary ushered them into Haden's office. Mr Haden approached her with a beaming smile and took her hand. 'Dr Barrett, how lovely to see you.' He leant forward to kiss her on the cheek. 'I can't tell you how much we've appreciated your hard work in the time you've been with us. I'm sure things will get back to normal soon. New samples are being produced even as we speak. You can even collect them while you're here. Once the report is finalised, you can get back to your normal life and we can go ahead with plans for our product.'

Haden frowned at Simon as he spoke, a silent disapproving comment on his presence in the meeting. Simon studied his nails, appearing bored with the whole conversation.

'I'm happy to be involved, Mr Haden. As you know, the product has passed every test with flying colours.' Beth rushed on, acting on pure instinct. 'I was wondering if we needed to get independent testing done, as a precaution.'

She was watching for a reaction, and caught it in the flexing of his fingers on the coffee mug. He covered it by returning the mug to the desk. 'I don't see that as being necessary. Our labs are the top of the line. Any information they give us is completely comprehensive.'

'Of course,' Beth answered him with a smile. 'It's your call, Mr Haden. I was just asking.'

'Wonderful, now can we go over some of the preliminary results collated since the fire. I'd love to get your feedback.'

With another report and another box of slides tucked under her arm, Beth shook Haden's hand as he saw them to the door several hours later. 'Let us know when you're ready, and we'll collect your data.' He peered at the clock on the wall. 'Forgive me, I didn't mean to keep you so late.'

'I didn't mind. It's good to be working again.'

As they passed reception, Beth spied a familiar face. 'Tim? What are you doing here? I was going to ring you and see if you needed a work reference. Simon, this is my lab assistant. I haven't heard from him since the fire.'

'I'm working. Mr Haden was kind enough to give me a position here at head office, coordinating another project.'

'That's great news. You deserve the promotion.'

'If *you* need any extra help, Dr Barrett, you know I'm always available.'

'Thank you. I think I can finalise things from home.'

'Well, you have my number if you need me.' He gave her an awkward pat on the shoulder before gesturing with his empty coffee cup and heading down the corridor.

'Does everyone love you?' Simon murmured, as they continued their exit out of the main doors. 'Of course they do.'

'Be quiet.' She nudged him in the ribs with her elbow.

'I notice you still didn't admit the independent labs to Haden.'

Beth nibbled on her fingernail. 'I don't even feel guilty. He reacted to my question about it, did you see?'

'I did.'

'It's not your paranoid delusions rubbing off on me?'

'It is not.' Simon crossed to the Ferrari's driver side. Beth gave him a warning glare. He raised his hands in capitulation and walked to the passenger side instead. He fiddled with the radio while she drove, landing on a classic rock station.

The trip progressed in blissful calm, until Simon began to tweak the wing mirror on his side.

'Will you stop that, you're creating a blind spot.'

'Red, honey, could you put your foot down, just a bit?'

'I'm doing the speed limit.'

'Humour me, just this once. Give her a little gas, then ease up.'

Beth did as he asked, sneaking a look when he remained silent. 'What's wrong?'

'I think we have a tail.'

'A what?'

'Someone's following us. When we sped up, so did they.'

Beth looked in the rear view mirror to see car lights some distance back. The country roads and lack of street lighting made further identification impossible. 'What do you want me to do?'

'Same as before.'

Beth planted her foot with more force, letting the car have its head for a few hundred yards, then easing back. Another peek in the mirror confirmed the sedan was keeping pace.

'We need to change this up and follow them.' Simon's voice was calm and cool, still watching the other vehicle in the side mirror.

'How?'

'Take the corner *now*.' Simon's barked command was so unexpected, Beth swung the wheel, taking the corner way too fast with a squeal of brakes. A dark-coloured sedan shot past them seconds later.

'Do a one-eighty, Red, quick – no, don't do a three-point turn, just *go*.'

Beth cursed under her breath as she jerked the car into a tight turn, bumping the curb in her haste.

'Faster would be better, sweetheart.'

Beth glowered at him. 'I suppose you want to drive.'

'No time to change. Go, I'll direct you on how to get the most out of this baby.' He turned to grin at her. 'Trust me, just floor it.'

'Only if you stop calling my car *baby*.' She slammed her foot down on the accelerator and the Ferrari shot forward. She swung back onto the road without indicating.

Simon's voice was constant. 'Look, there they are up ahead. Now we're in the driver's seat, so to speak. Power, give her more power, put your foot down. Change up. No, don't slow down for the corner. You'll lose them.'

She gritted her teeth as the powerful car surged ahead.

'Darn it, they've seen us. Look at them speeding up. Floor it, Red.' The dark car put on its indicators, but raced straight past the street instead of turning.

'They know there's a town up ahead. They're going to try to lose us in traffic instead of taking the back roads. Listen to me and do what I say, okay?'

'Okay.' She was light years away from okay. The car was too powerful beneath her hands and they were moving too fast.

'They'll try to lose us on side streets and they won't give any indication before they turn, so be ready, honey.' Simon's voice was calm and controlled. He was focused on the other car.

'Left, *left*!' Simon's shouted command made her jump. She saw no evidence of the sedan planning to turn, then it swerved and took a corner way too fast, and she followed, heart pumping.

'Good girl. *Right*, turn right.'

The car swerved again, and she followed. They were coming up to a stop sign and Beth slowed.

'Go through.'

'I can't.'

'They won't stop. It's fine. It's clear. Go through.' Sure enough, the sedan raced through the stop sign without pause.

Beth followed, holding her breath as she ran the intersection.

They approached traffic. The sedan swerved into another lane, causing a driver to honk his car horn and yell out of the window.

'Follow,' Simon instructed, and Beth gritted her teeth again, swinging into the next lane. The same driver honked again and hurled abuse at her.

The dark car took a sudden side street, and Beth swung into it without Simon's instruction.

'Good girl.' There was pride in his voice as they raced down the narrow road.

Another stop sign loomed ahead, at a much busier intersection. Beth couldn't bring herself to go through it.

The driver of the sedan didn't hesitate, causing cars to skid, two of them to narrowly avoid hitting each other.

She slowed down.

'Go, go, *go*!'

'I can't,' she yelled back to him.

'You can do this. Look, it's clear. Just go, honey, go.'

She sucked in a shuddering breath and raced through the intersection. A squeal of brakes echoed around her, changing pitch with a Doppler effect as she kept going.

Flashing lights up ahead signaled train crossing gates. Under any other circumstances, Beth would have rolled her eyes. *Oh for goodness' sake, what next? This is like a bad car chase movie.*

The gates started to close. The sedan sped up.

'Go, Red.'

She couldn't do it. Every instinct screamed at her not to rush the gates before they shut. This was a train, for heaven's sake. When trains and cars collided, trains always won.

The sedan flew through the closing boom gates, narrowly missing them, and sped off into the distance.

Beth slowed the car. Pulling into a side street, she put a shaky hand to the ignition and switched it off. Her racing heart and ragged breath were a physical pain in her chest.

Simon sighed into the silence. 'We would have made it.'

ೞ

'Is there any more information you can give me?' Jared asked over the phone.

'No that's it, a black Volvo sedan with tinted windows driving in the dark.' Simon ran his hand through his hair in frustration. He kept his voice low to avoid scaring the woman driving with steely concentration beside him.

'Plates?'

'Unreadable. I suspect they were coated in a reflective paint for just that purpose.'

'How is Dr Barrett?'

Simon studied Beth, driving at much less than the speed limit, her hands clenched on the wheel. 'Shaken.'

'With good reason. I'll put out a bulletin with our people, Simon, but I don't hold out much hope. Do you wish to contact the police?'

Simon blew out a breath. 'And say what? We think a sedan was following us, so we followed it instead? We have zero proof, Jared. The police will do nothing.'

Jared remained silent as they both knew Simon was right. 'It's so bloody frustrating, I know something is going on, but I can't figure out what.'

'You should take Dr Barrett to a hotel if you feel her house has been compromised.'

'I'm trying. She's as stubborn as Cec.'

'Do not shorten my wife's name.'

'She likes it.'

'I don't.'

'Give Cec a kiss. Tell her it's from me.'

'Over your dead body.'

Simon smiled, accepting the banter as their way of lessening a tense situation. 'Pull the surveillance on the house, Jared. Send the team to Haden's office instead.'

'As you wish. You are going to remove Dr Barrett from her home?'

'I'm going to damn well try.'

Simon hung up as Beth stopped the car in the street outside her house. Even in the moonlight, he could see the pulse beating wildly at her throat. His brave scientist was running on pure adrenaline and probably only moments from a full meltdown. They needed to go inside, pack a bag and head to a hotel. First, he needed to calm her down.

'That was fun, wasn't it?'

'No.'

'You've got a tight grip going on there, Red. Are you imagining that steering wheel is my throat?'

'Yes, it's amazingly satisfying.'

'I see.' He paused. 'It was a bit fun, really, if you think about it, and by the way, remarkable driving.'

Beth turned her head to glower at him. 'You really are clearly insane.' Taking both hands off the wheel, she waved them. 'No one, and I mean no one, could come away from this night with a feeling of fun. My heart is beating so fast I can't breathe. My hands are shaking, my legs are quivering. How is this *fun*?'

Her voice had risen with every syllable, and Simon was sure she'd forgotten they were parked under a tree outside her house at night. In a convertible. With the roof down.

'Okay, maybe fun isn't the right word. What about exciting? It's exciting, isn't it? Can't you sense the blood rushing through your veins? The adrenaline coursing through your system? Don't you feel a little bit more alive? And truthfully, don't you feel just a little bit – aroused?'

He said the words to calm her, to distract her. *And okay, maybe just because it's fun to tease her.*

Beth gaped at him, and Simon knew he'd gone too far. 'I'm sorry. Come on, let's go inside. I'll make some tea—'

She leapt – clambered was probably a better word – from her seat to his. He heard a whack and winced in sympathy as her knee struck the hand-brake during the clambering process. Simon barely had time to form a thought before she was on top of him, straddling his lap.

'Umm, Red?'

'Shut up.' Putting her hands on his face, she crushed her mouth to his, at the same time lowering her body and beginning to undulate.

The physical effect on Simon was immediate, and downright painful considering the slim cut of his trousers. She continued rubbing herself against him, moving backward and forward. Simon could do nothing except fight the physical waves of desire surging through his body. His seatbelt was still fastened, effectively trapping him in place.

He managed to get a small amount of space between his lips and hers. 'Red, honey, I don't think you've thought this through. I mean, there isn't a lot of room—'

'Shut up, Simon, just shut up.' Taking her hands from his face, she reached for his belt. Raising her body, she unfastened the buckle. As it came free, she tried to tug down his trousers. A tricky manoeuvre in the tight space.

Simon, fighting the growing arousal, gave logic one last try. 'Sweetheart? About ten feet from here is a nice bed, a really nice bed. Or a comfy sofa. Or if you're that impatient, the colourful rug you have *just* inside the front door.'

'Simon. For God's sake, stop complaining and *help* me.'

Logic lost, smothered by the breathless passion in her voice and the touch of her skin, he fumbled to unfasten his seatbelt then raised his hips to give her access to his trousers. She yanked them down, scouring his skin with her nails in her haste, and making him shudder. The clothing bunched around his thighs, and the cool night air combined with the heat from her body hit his arousal like an erotic summer storm.

Beth tried to raise her body. The space was too restrictive. She sobbed out a breath of frustration and Simon reached down, grasped the sheer silk of her underwear and yanked. Beth gasped as the delicate material came away from her body in shreds. Simon tossed the tattered silk aside, not knowing nor caring where it landed.

'Better,' he murmured against her lips.

'Much better.' Her whispered echo zinged along Simon's spine.

He put his hand on her back to steady her and leant forward. The change of position brought their bodies closer together, and she shuddered at the intimate contact. With his free hand, he searched for the catch on the glove box until it sprang open. He reached in and removed a small box, then reached inside the box and removed a silver packet.

Her beautiful eyes widened when he brought the packet around to tear it open with his teeth.

'Condoms? Who keeps condoms in the glove box of their car? Wait a minute, this is *my* car. Why are there condoms in the glove box of my car?'

'We could go inside and discuss it.'

'Shut up, Simon.' She silenced him with her mouth.

Simon had no idea how long they continued like this. The night stole all sense of time. All that existed was the small sounds and murmurs of their voices, and the increased harshness of their breathing as desire took control.

This is insane. It was the last coherent thought Simon had.

When the passionate storm passed, he clung to her until his breathing returned to normal.

His sexy scientist – of course – recovered first.

'Oh my God.'

'No argument from me, Red.' He murmured the reply against her skin.

'We're making love in a car! A car with no roof, outside my *house*.' She clamped her hands over her mouth, her tone dipping to a horrified whisper. 'What if my neighbours heard?'

Grinning and tugging her fingers away, Simon kissed them and put his own hands on her cheeks. 'Sweetheart,

I assure you the moans of pleasure coming from that sweet mouth were music to my ears only and not nearly loud enough for anyone else to hear.'

He peered at the dark houses surrounding them, put a finger to her lips, and whispered, 'Having said that, it's likely they just heard your *announcement* of us making love.'

Beth hid her face in his neck and groaned, the heat of her blush burning his skin.

'You are such a bad influence.'

Simon chuckled. 'You know, it's funny how many people say that.'

Chapter 5

Sleep released its grip with slow reluctance. Surreal dreams became memories. Images of the previous night's evocative encounter flickered behind his eyelids like sensual snapshots, tempting his mind and body to consciousness with promises of an encore performance.

Beth wriggled, and Simon moved his hand to her hip to caress the soft skin.

'Simon, you're lying on my hair.'

He stroked his hand back and forth. 'I like your hair. It always smells like orange blossom.'

'You're stopping me from getting out of the bed.'

'Good, I don't want you to get out of the bed.'

'Simon!' She wriggled again.

So much for my seduction techniques.

Realising her need for leaving him was probably a trip to the bathroom that she didn't want to vocalise, Simon raised his head without opening his eyes, allowing her to slide her hair free. He managed to pinch her bottom as she slipped from the bed, making her yelp.

Still with his eyes closed, Simon shuffled to her side of the bed, inhaling the sweet scent of her that clung to the pillow, the sheets, to him.

They needed to go. They should have left last night, before the erotic experience in the Ferrari put an entirely different spin to the evening. Simon grinned as he breathed in the lingering smell of orange blossom on fine cotton. Making love in a car was one thing. Attempting to disengage oneself from said vehicle with modesty and dignity was quite another. He could still see the flush on her cheeks even the moonlight could not disguise.

However, his sensual scientist had slept soundly in his arms, with no trace of stress from her car chase experience.

Pushing aside a vision of silken arms and legs wrapped around his body and the kiss of the night air on naked skin, Simon forced his brain to concentrate, to make plans. They'd pack a simple bag and be on their way. The microscope and slides were with Bryce, so no need for Beth to worry about her work. Anything else she needed, he would buy. Clothes, toiletries ... the world, moon and stars.

Focus.

He'd pick a top quality hotel, the very best. Her necessary incarceration shouldn't be a hardship. Simon knew of one in the city with excellent security and a fantastic presidential suite. Not to mention a bath big enough to play in and a king-size bed.

Focus!

Maybe they didn't need to be in England. Jared had a townhouse in Paris, the city of love and romance.

God Dammit. Sighing at the sensual imagery that refused to go away, Simon opened his eyes. 'Red?'

'I'll be back in a minute.' Her voice came from along the hallway.

Simon's stomach rumbled. They'd both missed dinner the night before. Should they have breakfast here before heading out?

Back?

He bolted upright. 'Back from where?'

'I'm just going to put the car in the garage. I know we put the roof up, but what if someone scratches it?' Her voice faded and Simon heard a clinking sound, like someone grabbing car keys from a glass coffee table.

Simon's words to Jared came back to haunt him. *Pull the surveillance from the house.*

Alarm bells went off in his head. 'Beth, no, don't go outside.' Launching himself from the bed, Simon heard the front door open.

'Beth, stop!'

She was a few steps from the door and turned her head at the sound of his voice. He saw to his horror she was aiming the car remote. 'Don't press that.'

'What?' She frowned in confusion. Her thumb automatically finished the action.

The car exploded in a ball of flame.

'Beth!'

The force of the blast threw her backward, sending her sprawling onto the cobbled footpath. Simon reached her in a split second, yanking her back inside and slamming the door shut.

'Christ, are you all right? Can you hear me? Are you hurt?' He kept them at a low crouch, away from the windows, some of which were miraculously unbroken. Blood marred the skin of her neck and forehead, and Simon raised a shaking finger to her face. 'Are you in pain? God, Red, please talk to me.'

She blinked at him, eyes blank with shock. 'You're naked.'

'And you could have been killed.' Stopping his frantic check for injuries for one second, he pulled her close to his body while his mind played horrible scenarios of what would have happened if she'd been closer to the car before pressing the remote.

The sound of sirens pulled him back to the situation in hand. People outside were yelling in confusion and fear. Simon had no idea how much damage the explosion had caused to the surrounding houses.

He shook off his mental turmoil and put his hands to the sides of her face to get her attention. 'We have to go.'

'Go?' Her expression remained blank.

Simon had no idea if the culprits were hanging around to make sure Beth went up with the car and he had no intention of finding out. If they knew she'd escaped, there was a chance the house would be the next target. He needed to use the mass confusion to get them out right now.

'Beth, I need you to go and get changed.'

'Okay … into what?'

Simon kissed her forehead. 'Jeans and a T-shirt. Just hurry please.'

Racing into the bedroom with her, Simon yanked on his trousers and shoes from last night. He cracked the curtain and peered outside. The police had arrived. *Why are they always on time when you don't want them to be?* An older woman in a dressing gown was gesturing and pointing to her door.

Simon considered his options. Should they go with the police and trust them to keep them safe? He'd always found that when it came to staying alive, the old catchphrase of *trust no one* had stood him in good stead.

'Simon?' Beth was standing by the wardrobe door, her shirt sitting haphazardly on her jeans-clad body, her feet jammed into ballet flats.

'Do you trust me?' he asked.

'Yes.'

'Okay then, let's go.'

They raced out the back door and through the rear gate. Simon took advantage of the chaos outside to slip down the side street, pulling out his phone. 'Jared, we need a pickup.'

'When?'

'Five minutes ago.'

'Where?'

'Beth's house.'

'I thought you were going to leave.'

'No time to argue, time is of the essence.'

'Wait.' A tapping sound meant Jared was checking the location of their people. 'Jade is the closest in proximity. Ten to fifteen minutes is the best I can do. Wait at the junction by the rear lane.'

'Understood.'

'Do I need to send someone to Dr Barrett's house?'

'Yes.' Anger was taking control of his emotions. 'Tell them to kill anyone who looks suspicious, probably *not* the policemen.' He hung up without elaborating. Jared could yell at him later.

Simon pulled a trembling Beth into the shadow of a large tree, scanning the area. Ten to fifteen minutes can seem like a lifetime when your life is in danger.

A silver Mercedes turned the corner and stopped. Simon urged Beth inside, aware she was barely conscious of anything currently happening. 'Good to see you, Two-Jay.'

She pulled back into traffic. 'Where are we going?'

'Mayfair.'

'Your place?' Her gaze met his in the rearview mirror. Jade knew his rules. No one involved in a mission ever went to Simon's private residence.

Simon put his arms around Beth, pulling her into his chest. 'My place, and step on it.'

༄

Beth couldn't stop her body from shaking no matter how hard she tried. She ran her fingers along the dark glass of the dining table. Italian designed if she had to guess, expensive too. A plate sat in front of her holding the remains of a sandwich. The china was black with gold trim. A matching mug sat beside it. Beth nudged the mug an inch to the left, so it lined up with the plate. Jade had brought food to the apartment then left. Beth couldn't remember when that all happened. Had it been an hour ago? Two hours? Ten minutes?

Turning her attention to the other side of the room, she saw her protector talking quietly on the phone. This was Simon the hunter, the warrior. Lighthearted, playful Simon was gone for now, and she didn't want to disturb his concentration or appear weak. He was trying to save her life and she wouldn't let him down.

Standing up from the table, Beth wondered what to do next. Her thought process was muddled, and she was cold. Shock maybe? She tried to think of the symptoms of shock, forcing her brain to work, to think logically. Then she asked herself *why* she was trying to think logically and wondered if that was shock too.

A long white couch in soft leather sat in the centre of the room. Beth ran her hands along the back. The cuff of Simon's shirt brushed her fingers. How had his shirt gotten on her body? Beth had a momentary blank before a memory returned of him slipping her limp arms through the sleeves, saying something about blood on her T-shirt. Raising her fingers to her face, Beth touched the Band-Aids covering the shallow cuts in two spots. Images slammed into her brain. The force of the explosion, the heat of the flames.

Beth sank to the ground, her back to the couch. Trying not to think of anything, she let the tears come.

'Hey.'

Lifting her head from her folded arms and drawn-up knees, Beth watched through bleary eyes as Simon sat down in front of her. There was so much compassion on his face. 'Did anyone die? In my street?'

'No. The explosion was precise, designed to dispose of the person inside the car only. Your neighbors have a few broken windows and a lot to gossip about, but no one is hurt. Not one single person.'

Tears pricked her eyes again. 'Thank God. I don't think I could have lived with myself. How will you explain what happened?'

'Jared is handling it. Don't worry.'

'Simon.' She hesitated, and the next words came out in a whisper. 'Someone wants me dead, and I don't understand why.'

'I know, and I swear to you, I'll find out. Whoever is behind this will pay. Give me your hands.' He offered her his, palms up.

'Are we going somewhere?'

'No, just give me your hands.'

She wiped her cheeks and placed her damp fingers in his.

Simon interlinked their fingers. 'I want you to squeeze.'

Beth pressed down.

'No, really squeeze my hands tight, like you mean it.'

'I ... I might hurt you.'

'Doesn't matter.'

Gripping his fingers tighter, she squeezed until his signet ring bit into her flesh. For some reason, the small pain was calming. It was real, tangible.

'Good girl. Now breathe in deep, and as you exhale, concentrate on your grip on my hands. Concentrate on pushing all the stress from your body out along your arms, into your fingers and into me.'

Beth did as he instructed, inhaling until her lungs filled, then blowing out a breath and focusing on nothing except their joined hands.

'Again,' he ordered, and she repeated the ritual five more times. Until her fingers tingled from the pressure and her lungs complained at the enforced exercise. 'How do you feel?'

'Better.' Her voice held a hint of surprise because she *was* surprised. 'Where did you learn that?'

'It's one of Jared's tricks. Works every time. It's an okay method. I prefer mine. Come here.' Shuffling to her side, he leant against the sofa back and pulled her into his arms.

Beth released another, calmer breath. Her tingling fingers tangled in the fine cotton of his shirt. 'Thank you. I don't know what's wrong with me.'

'Nothing is wrong with you.' He kissed her forehead.

'It's like everything is too much.'

Simon reached up, grabbed the dark burgundy throw rug lying across the top of the couch and pulled it down, covering them from head to toe.

'What are you doing?'

'Sometimes, when the world seems too much, the simple solution is to create a smaller world. How's this?'

The soft rug shut out most of the light except a faint glimmer through the tight weave. The dark enclosed space brought with it a sense of calm. 'Much better.'

He pressed another kiss to her forehead. 'Welcome to Red World.'

'Sounds like we're on Mars.'

'Fair point. Winters' World?'

'Antarctica.'

He sighed in dramatic fashion. 'Barrett World, then. I challenge you to find something to complain about that.'

'Perfect.' She snuggled closer to his chest, the silly conversation calming her senses even more. 'How long can we stay in Barrett World?'

'As long as you want. As long as you need.'

'What do we do while we're here?'

'I don't know about you, but I'm going to do this.' Tilting her chin up with one finger, he brushed the lightest of kisses over her mouth.

'I liked it when Jared did that,' she murmured. 'It's very romantic.'

Simon pulled back, and even in the darkness she could see the frown on his face. 'Jared kissed you?'

'No, Jared kissed Cecilia.'

'Jared is always kissing Cecilia. That's okay then. If I'm not allowed to kiss his lady, he's certainly not allowed to kiss mine.'

While she was still digesting those words, he lowered his mouth to hers again.

When he had kissed her in the laneway, she told herself it wasn't real.

When he had kissed her in Jared's office, she told herself he'd just been teasing her.

When she'd seduced him in the car, she told herself she had instigated it. He hadn't had a choice.

This time she had no excuses, and he seemed determined that this time it was by his rules.

Simon tightened his arms around her back, lifting one hand to tangle in her hair. He deepened the kiss in tiny increments, first so soft he was barely touching her, then moving his lips ever so slowly over hers, using the tip of his tongue to outline her mouth.

Deeper and deeper, soft movements, teasing nibbling movements of his mouth on hers, but still not invading it. She told herself it should have been a chaste kiss, but in fact, it was the most sensual thing she had ever experienced. And exactly what she needed.

Simon's hand was still twisted in her hair. He moved it down to caress the back of her neck. Lifting his mouth from hers, he nuzzled her neck and whispered in her ear, 'We haven't done things in the proper order, have we? I thought we'd go back a few steps. I'm only going to kiss you. If it's too much, tell me, and I'll stop.'

'I don't want you to stop.'

How long they stayed there, she couldn't tell. Light, teasing kisses stole the seconds away and pulled the residual tension from her body. When he cradled her head on his shoulder, she was wrung out, exhausted.

'Rest, my brave little scientist. Barrett World isn't going anywhere, and neither am I.'

Beth closed her eyes, and in the dappled light of their enclosed space and surrounded by Simon's strong arms, she slept.

ꝏ

Simon turned from the stove as he heard the bathroom door open. Beth padded toward him clad in another of his shirts, a soft green that highlighted her eyes. She still wore her jeans, and her feet were bare. A fluffy white towel shrouded her hair.

'Better?'

'Thank you, yes. Your apartment is extraordinary.'

'I'm glad you approve. You may be here for a while.' He peeled the damp Band-Aids from her face and touched the small wounds. The scratches weren't deep and should heal without a scar. Simon replaced them with clean dressings and kissed each spot. 'I died a thousand deaths when that explosion happened, and it was a wakeup call. Everything I've done has put you in danger. From now on, you stay here, where it's safe.'

Beth placed her hands on his forearms. 'You had no idea this would happen.'

'I should have. I've been an impulsive fool. It stops now.'

'Are you becoming responsible?' Her tone had a teasing edge, and it made Simon's heart swell with pride to see her spirit recovering.

'As much as I hate to admit it, yes, I believe I am. Sit down, Dr Barrett. I'll brush out the tangles in your hair.'

Returning from the bathroom with a bristle brush, he unwound the towel from her head and started to work his way through the thick, wet curls.

'Simon, why did you become an agent?'

'I don't remember. It was a long time ago.'

'Can you talk about what you do? Not the secrets, I mean, just some of your adventures? I need a distraction.'

'How do you know I've had adventures?'

Beth laughed. The sound zinged like a lightning bolt along Simon's body and landed firmly in his groin.

He gave an exaggerated, heartfelt sigh. 'Fine, you sit there and relax, and I'll talk.'

'So I tied him to the camel.'

'You're making this up.'

'I am not.' He put as much indignity as he could in his voice and was rewarded by another light, tinkling laugh.

'That's ridiculous. There's no *way* that's all true. And I can't believe I'm laughing after everything that's happened to me lately. My boss is probably corrupt, my lab caught fire and my car blew up. Am I having a breakdown?'

'Not a breakdown. The brain copes with stress by focusing on the positives. You can do it because you're strong.'

She shook her head. 'I'm not.'

'Sweetheart, you're the strongest person I know.' She turned in the chair, and Simon lost himself in that strength and beauty. Something primal and protective curled deep in his gut. *How am I ever going to let this woman go?* 'Will you sit still? I can't reach your hair if you wriggle. Anyway, as I was saying, then the helicopter arrived, and you have no idea how happy I was to wave my mission goodbye, even if it did mean I had to trek another three days to civilisation,' he concluded his story with a final sweep of the hairbrush.

'I have a question.'

'Ask me anything.'

'How did condoms get in the glove box of my car?'

'Mild change of subject then. I wondered if we'd get to that.'

She turned in the chair again to watch him, her expression serious. A lock of drying hair fell over her shoulder. Simon picked up the curl and played with it. 'I didn't plan to seduce you, but as a scientist, you have to understand the concept of chemistry. We have it, a lot of it.'

She flushed and nodded.

'When I went grocery shopping, I saw the box and bought it. I was being a responsible adult, with no expectations. I put them in the glovebox, so you didn't get embarrassed when unpacking the bags. I tried slipping them into my shirt pocket, it created an unsightly bulge. Fashion wise, I simply couldn't do it.' Simon lowered his voice to a dramatic whisper. 'My years of secret agent training finally paid off. As it turns out, the glove box was *exactly* where the condoms needed to be.'

She flushed a brilliant red to rival her hair and stumbled to her feet with a murmured groan.

Simon wrapped his arms around her before she could escape and soothed his next words by running a hand down her back. 'I know you're upset about your car, Red, but you have to admit, we gave it a great send off.'

A startled giggle escaped her as Simon had hoped. 'I've been thinking,' he added. 'When this drama is all over, I wondered if we could talk.'

The phone rang, and she jerked at the sound. 'You should get that. It might be Jared.'

'Jared wouldn't use the land line. The machine will take it.'

'*Simon, darling.*' Simon smiled at the voice coming from the recorder before realising Beth had tensed completely, her spine rigid. She tried to move. He held her in place.

'*We hope to see you next week. Your sister said if you miss the birth of your latest nephew, she will hunt you down. Ring your mother occasionally, my darling boy. Let me know you're well.*'

Beth stirred as the call ended. 'That was your mum.'

'It was, and you assumed my lover was calling me while I had you wrapped in my arms.'

'I didn't think that.'

'Liar. Shame on you, Dr Barrett.' He whispered the last words in her ear, while she squirmed.

'Are you close to your family?' Her voice was tantalisingly husky.

'Incredibly.'

'Do they know what you do?'

'I suspect my parents have put the pieces together over the years. My sisters think I work as a consultant for an international finance company.' Simon stroked Beth's cheek. 'I know you lost your parents young. Mine would love you. Perhaps when this is over, we could talk?'

The doorbell rang, and Beth's muscles locked up. Simon swore under his breath. *Is there no end to these interruptions today? All I want to do is ask her out on a damn date.* 'Relax.' He kissed her mouth. 'It's probably Bryce. Stay here while I check.'

'Were you followed?'

'Don't be an idiot.' Bryce strode past him.

'That would be a no then?'

Bryce crossed to Beth. 'I have your scope ready and decided it was safer to deliver it myself. Simon thought you might need something to take your mind off things. Are you all right?'

'A little better, thank you. Did you really fix it?'

'You'll find it adequate for the short term. Give me a week once this is all over and it will be as good as new. You have my word.'

Simon watched as Beth pulled the instrument from the container together with the sample box. She set it up on his dining table, eagerness and anticipation in her every move. 'This is amazing,' she said with her eye to the lens. 'Truly amazing. I had no idea this was possible, and to do it in such a short time.'

'Thank you. I enjoyed it. I'm not on active duty right now. I needed a challenge.'

Beth raised her head. 'What happened?'

'Coincidently, mine was a lab accident too. I inhaled some noxious fumes, impairing my lung capacity.' Bryce shrugged. 'It's fine as long as I don't exert myself.'

He made it sound so trivial, when in fact, he'd been caught in a massive chemical explosion and pulled three people to safety before the fire trucks arrived.

I'm not going to say anything to make him even more heroic in Beth's eyes.

'I know what you mean.' Beth placed her hand on her own chest. 'It feels odd, doesn't it? Like tightness in your lungs.'

'Exactly. Like being at high altitude.'

'Yes, that's just how mine feel.' She smiled at him.

Simon folded his arms. *Great, now they have something else in common.* 'I know you're all super secretive about this, but I filled Jet in on what you're doing.'

Beth glanced first at Simon, then at Bryce. 'Of course, I guess keeping the secret is redundant now.'

'Do you know which test results have come back so far?' Bryce asked.

'Mainly chemical substance tests. Corrosion, degradation after exposure, things like that. Everything's been perfect. No flaws, no changes to the fibres.'

'Do you have comparative tests between the independent labs and the Haden labs yet? The same tests completed by both?'

'Not yet. I'm expecting some in the next batch. Both were testing heat and cold. The Haden labs came back perfect so the comparisons will be vital. They're probably ready to be collected today.'

Simon handed her his laptop. 'Use this to check your messages, not your phone. This server is more secure.'

She logged on and shook her head at the screen. 'My main email account is *full* of messages.'

Bryce leant on the table and crossed his arms. 'Comparative testing is the best option you have regarding proof. If Haden is hiding something, they'll falsify their lab results, but they won't be able to tamper with independent ones. If I can help in any way, let me know.'

'Thank you, Bryce.' She threw her arms around his neck in a full-on hug. 'You're a good friend.'

Simon showed him to the door and tried to be civil. It wasn't Bryce's fault he had more in common with Beth than he did. 'Thanks for coming out.'

'You're welcome.' He peered at his beeping phone. 'Looks like Jared's trying to reach you. Better give him a call. Oh, and Simon? Don't be an idiot. I'm not trying to steal your girl.'

'She isn't my girl.'

'I take it back. You are an idiot.' With a careless wave, Bryce strode back to his car.

Simon turned to the woman occupying his every thought, to the sure and certain knowledge he'd ceased to exist in her eyes.

Beth had her eye to her scope, her body language a study in deep concentration. He placed a kiss on her hair, making her jump. 'I thought you were checking your emails?'

'They're still downloading.' Her answer was mumbled, it was obvious where her true focus was.

He pressed another kiss to her cheek. 'Enjoy your repaired microscope, Red.' As soon as he was out of earshot, he called Jared. 'You have news?'

'Something unexpected. The authorities found the remains of drugs and money in the boot of the Ferrari. A considerable quantity of both.'

'*What?*'

'I take it you think they were planted?'

'Bloody hell, Jared. She's not a drug dealer, of course they were planted.'

'You need to keep a low profile. The police are searching for Dr Barrett, and the media has already picked up the story.'

Beth's emails. *Christ*. 'I'll call you back.'

'Don't check your messages—'

Too late. He knew the moment he saw her face. The tears streaming down her cheeks were highlighted from the glare of the laptop's screen. 'I ... I didn't do this. I didn't deal drugs. Simon, why would they say such a thing. It's not true, I *swear* it's not true.'

'I know. I know, Red.' He folded her in his arms.

'There's an email from the Scientific Institute. They want their award back "under the circumstances". I had no idea what they meant, so I checked the news site, and I'm on there. They have my picture. They all do, all the news sites. It's everywhere, Simon, *everywhere.*'

'It's a setup, and a successful one.' Simon reached over and slammed the laptop shut.

'What do we do?'

'First, I need to call Jared back to get some more details. Do you want to listen in?'

She shook her head.

'Are you sure?'

'Do what you need to do. I'll ... I'll cook dinner.' Swiping the tears from her cheeks, she strode into the kitchen, spine straight, head held high.

Simon reached for his phone to continue his conversation, fighting off wave after wave of anger.

'The authorities are still an obvious presence at the house,' Jared said. 'It would be foolish for the perpetrators to attempt a break-in to plant more false evidence with police combing the area. How is Dr Barrett holding up this time?'

'Better than half the agents I know. She's so strong, Jared, so bloody brave.' Simon could hear the pride in his voice. 'Trained operatives would have cracked by now, not her.' He ran a hand through his hair. 'What I don't understand is, if it is Haden, why hire us to protect her, *then* try to kill her?'

'It's the perfect alibi. Haden will tell everyone although they took every step to protect her, she died despite their best efforts. It reinforces any results they wish to publish. Legitimate proof they have nothing to hide. A simple and clever plan.'

Simon could barely contain the burning rage in his gut. 'I want to kill them.'

'Go right ahead.' Jared's unruffled tone didn't change. 'However, first let us find out *who* we have to kill and why someone is so determined to blacken Dr Barrett's reputation.'

'Did Haden ask for us specifically?'

'No, Jade picked the assignment off the system because it fit your criteria. I made sure it was allocated to us.'

No one knew exactly how Jared procured missions. Simon suspected he had links to sources worldwide.

'Haden knows nothing about us, then. He thinks I'm a standard bodyguard.'

'He does. I suggest you use that to your advantage. Can you think of anyone else who may be involved? We need to cover all our bases.'

'There's some jerk, a former boyfriend. You could check him out. And three women, award nominees, who were all at the awards night. They seemed nice, but maybe jealousy is involved?' Simon rattled off the names as far as he knew them.

'Leave it with me.'

Beth was still in his kitchen when he returned to her.

'What did Jared say?' She didn't turn around.

'He's looking into everything.'

'Good, that's good.' After a moment of silence, she finally spun to face him, a razor sharp boning knife held in her hands. 'You do believe me, don't you?'

Simon placed both hands on her shoulders. 'I do, and I would, even if you weren't armed with a deadly weapon.'

The flicker of confusion on her face morphed into a wry half-smile as he plucked the blade from her white-knuckled grip. 'I think I'm a little tense.'

'Only a little? I'm one heartbeat away from a mental breakdown and you're chopping vegies with a fish knife. I'd say we both need a diversion. Something to take our mind off this chaos and mayhem.'

The all too familiar blush stained her cheeks a dusky rose. 'What sort of diversion?'

Simon refused to let his mind drift into sensual territory. As much as he wanted Beth back in his bed, it had to be for the right reasons. He dropped his voice to a whisper. 'Take- away pizza and a movie.'

Beth fell asleep with her head in his lap before the second rom-com hero/heroine got to their happy ending. Her warm breath was an erotic torture on his thigh even through the fine wool blend of his slacks. Simon eased out from under her, propping her head up with a cushion. She muttered in her sleep, but didn't stir.

Padding to the kitchen in bare feet, he called the office, knowing darn well Jared would still be there. 'Update?'

'You were right about the former boyfriend.'

Hope and anger fought for control of Simon's emotions. 'He's in on all this?'

'No, he's a jerk, posting vague, insulting comments about Dr Barrett's eccentricities and lack of dating skills on various social media platforms. Unfortunately, he's just a jerk and not a suspect.'

Simon gripped the phone until it creaked in his hand. 'Are you sure? I'd be happy to take him down anyway.'

'I wouldn't worry about it. Bryce appears to have accidentally deleted or compromised *all* of his accounts, and not just the social media ones. I'm certain the red tape and system errors regarding Mr Weaver's bank accounts and utility bills will keep him too busy to bother Dr Barrett any further.'

Simon made a mental note to high five Jet for his ingenuity, once this was all over.

Jared continued, 'All her other friends and colleagues, including the other award nominees, appear more supportive and ready to discount the alleged crimes leveled against her, if their various postings are to be believed.'

'Which brings us back to Haden.' Simon yanked at his hair. 'It's textiles, Jared. What could be so important?'

'In my experience, it tends to come down to warfare. Ask Beth if there are military applications for the product. There's always money in war. I'll call you if I have any further updates.'

War. Simon hung up and stared at the picture on his wall, running ideas through his mind. The painting depicted a Samurai warrior in full armour.

Armour. The answer slammed into his mind with stunning clarity.

'Simon?' Beth stood in the doorway, her eyes still blurry from sleep.

Simon folded her in his arms. 'Sweetheart, I know your mind is spiraling with stress right now, and I'd rather be discussing other things, but you and I need to talk about war.'

'War?'

'Military. What sort of military applications could these textiles have?'

'I have no idea.'

'Tell me again, what does this fabric look like when it's more than a half-inch square?'

'It's just fabric, a lightweight, super-strong fabric, you wouldn't guess its strength by looking at it.'

'I have a crazy theory, Red. I've been looking at this the wrong way. Bryce is right, I am an idiot, and not only about you and him.'

'What about me and him?'

'This is the answer. It *has* to be.'

'Simon, stop talking in riddles. I'm barely awake, and you're making my head spin even more.'

'Body armour, Red. Tough, light fabric soldiers could wear for protection without weight or impairment of movement. If it's as strong as you say, then it's the perfect next step up from existing tactical wear. Anyone marketing this would be instantly rich, unless—'

'Unless the textile is faulty,' she finished for him.

'Then all that nice marketing potential and massive financial returns go down the drain. We need that next lot of lab results. Can we check your other email address?'

The confirmation message from the post office had arrived the day before. Simon tapped the screen. 'I know you wanted to keep this totally anonymous. I think that ship's sailed. What if we could pick up the results from your secret post office box instead of involving a courier?'

She nodded her agreement. 'To hell with anonymity. Do it. What about a car?'

Simon pulled her close for a long kiss, certain they were on the right track and once again humbled by her strength and resilience. 'We're in my home now. My other cars are downstairs. The police are looking for you, sweetheart, I need you to stay here where you're safe. Give me directions and I'll do the collecting.'

'Okay.' She scowled at him. 'Hold on. That's a dirty trick. You kiss me and I end up agreeing with whatever you say. How is that fair?'

'Because you're stubborn, and I need every advantage I can get?'

'Now you're buttering me up.'

'Interesting thought. Maybe I'll stop at the supermarket on the way back.'

She blinked and started to stammer. Simon pressed his advantage. 'Directions, Dr Barrett. To the post office, I mean, not for the butter. Do I need a key to the post office box?'

'A code, not a key, it's electronic.'

'Which you will write down for me, together with directions.' When she finished, he slipped the paper into his pocket. 'I'll be as quick as I can. Stay off the internet, you'll only upset yourself, don't check your phone messages, and do *not* move from this apartment. It's the most secure place you could be. Most of the people who live here need to feel safe. Sometimes for their political status, sometimes for the mistresses they keep in residence.'

'Is that supposed to reassure me?'

'It should.'

'Have you kept a mistress here?'

'The only woman who has seen inside this apartment is you, my sweet.' He kissed the tip of her nose. 'Don't spend all of your time peering into that microscope either.'

'Simon,' she called as he reached the door. 'Do you really think we're on to something?'

She looked so hopeful that once again Simon was overwhelmed by a surge of protective instinct, a burning desire to see her safe. 'I hope so, I really do.'

The apartment was dark when he returned. Putting the package on the table, Simon checked each room, finding Beth sprawled on his bed. The red duvet against her bright hair had transformed her into a pagan princess, her wild curls spread over his pillow.

Lying down beside her, he watched her sleep. Watched the gentle rise and fall of her body caused by each breath. How many days since they first met? Enough to fall in love? Their former boss had succumbed to true love over a series of phone messages. Jared had fallen head over heels with Cecilia after one glance in a crowded ballroom.

'A week or a lifetime, it wouldn't have made any difference. I'm all in, Red. Now we need a break in the chaos, so I can convince you to stay.'

Beth opened her eyes and gave him a lazy smile. 'Are you Simon Sprawling again?'

'Guilty, I only do it because I know you like it. I should have woken you, but you look beautiful lying there. I wanted to watch you for a while.' He stroked her cheek. 'I know life has been crazy and we only just met, but I wondered, when things calm down—'

She sat bolt upright. 'You're back. Did you get the samples?'

'Yes, they're on the table, but, I was about to say—' He reached for her. She evaded his hand and scrambled off the bed.

'This could give us the answers, Simon. This could be the end of everything.' She called the words over her shoulder as she flew from the room, her incredible flaming hair catching the light.

Rolling over, Simon inhaled the scent of that luscious hair lingering on his pillow. He placed his hand where her head had been, relishing the warmth captured in the cotton.

I'm in love with you, Dr Elizabeth Barrett, and I don't want this to be the end of everything.

Chapter 6

Beth unpacked all the samples and set them out on the table. Taking a pad and a pen, she created three columns.

'Exposure to cold. Sample one, laboratory two. Test number D4K1. Result positive.' She put a tick beside her notes.

'Exposure to caustic chemicals. Sample three, laboratory two. Test number H7M5. Result positive.' Another tick.

An hour later she lifted her head and stretched out her neck. Nothing. She reached for the next box.

'Exposure to heat. Sample twelve, laboratory one ...'

On and on it went, until her eyes began to blur and the muscles in her lower back were begging for mercy. She couldn't give up. She *wouldn't* give up. Staring at the final sample, Beth huffed out a breath and pressed her tired eyes to the eyepiece lens. 'Exposure to heat. Sample nineteen, laboratory six. Test number K9D2. Result—'

Beth looked, and looked again. She stood, and had to grab the chair back as her leg muscles objected to the extended period of enforced inactivity. What time was it? 'Simon?' Her only reply was silence. The apartment was in full darkness. Rubbing her neck muscles, she fumbled her way back to the bedroom in the unfamiliar surroundings, and found him sleeping, his hand on the pillow where her head had rested.

My dangerous, brave, daredevil protector. Switching on the bedside lamp, she touched his shoulder. He stirred, blinking against the light. 'Sorry. I dozed off.' Something in her expression must have alerted him. 'What is it? What did you find?'

Her mind was in a daze. 'I tested everything twice.'

'And?' he prompted, rising on one elbow.

'We were right, the Haden labs and the independent ones have a discrepancy.'

'On which test?'

'Heat. The samples degrade after prolonged exposure to heat. The material loses eighty percent of its tensile strength.'

'Christ, that's huge. The majority of military conflict these days is conducted in hot climates.'

'You think Haden knows?'

'I'd bet every car in my garage he knows.' He cupped her chin in his hands. 'You found it, Red, you found the answer.'

'It isn't enough, especially now my reputation is in tatters. We need concrete evidence.'

'Such as?'

'Actual full-size examples of each fabric variation for further comprehensive testing.'

'Do you know where we'd find these full-size pieces?'

'I've only ever seen them at one place. Haden's main laboratories.'

'Great, let's go.'

'Now?'

'Right now.'

'That's impossible.'

He gave her one of those daredevil smiles. 'My darling Dr Barrett, don't you know me well enough by now to realise I consider nothing impossible?'

ಶಿ

Simon knocked on Bryce's front door. He used a specific rhythm. 'I don't know why I allowed you to come.'

Beth snorted. 'You didn't *allow* me to come. I insisted.'

'I thought we agreed you should stay at home where it's safe.'

'You agreed. I didn't. You need me to tell you what the textile looks like.'

'Red, you've been framed, you've been blown up. You were in tears only hours ago.'

Beth tilted her chin. 'You don't know the layout of the lab like I do. Besides, I want this over, I want this finished, so stop arguing.'

'You are one stubborn woman.' Simon knocked again. 'I'm beginning to understand how Jared feels.'

'Didn't you use a key to get in last time?'

'Most of the operatives have keys to each other's places, in case of emergencies. Jet has some pretty sophisticated security systems at night, and I didn't want to trip anything. I'm sure he's still awake.' Simon peered at his watch. 'Two am is early evening for Jet. Once he gets working on a project, he often stays up all night.'

The door opened to reveal a sleepy Bryce, wearing only a pair of low-slung track pants, rumpled hair and an annoyed expression.

Beth winced and whispered to Simon, 'I don't think he was still up.'

'Simon, why are you dragging Beth out in the middle of the night? Shouldn't she be at home, safe?' Bryce leant on the doorframe, one arm raised and his head resting on it. A lock of dark hair fell over his forehead, shadowing eyes of dark tawny gold highlighted by the porch light.

Bryce Black is a very handsome man. Beth's musings ended in a yelp as Simon poked her in the ribs.

'She's staying here. You and I need to break into Haden Corporation's secure laboratory.'

'Of course we do.' Bryce pushed away from the door, allowing them access. As he walked across the room, he raised one arm and crossed it over his shoulder, using the other to hold his elbow in a stretch. The movement caused the well-defined muscles in his back to ripple. Beth allowed her gaze to wander to the track pants sitting precariously low on slim hips.

'Ouch, Simon, will you stop poking me?'

'I thought you might be falling asleep. Jet, will you put some clothes on please?'

'Why?' Bryce asked.

'You can't go out like that.'

'I don't intend going anywhere until I have a coffee. Will you join me, Beth?'

'Yes.' Beth pulled away from Simon's arm around her waist and followed Bryce to the kitchen. A glance back told her Simon was glaring at her in disapproval.

'You're *not* coming with us.' He jabbed a finger in her direction.

'Yes, I am. Bryce will protect me.'

'*I'm* your protector.'

'Okay, you can come too.'

Simon scowled, and Bryce chuckled as he handed her a cup.

'Why did you bring guns?' Beth was whispering again.

'To keep you safe. It's in my job description.'

'I know, but *guns*?'

'Think of them as a necessary evil, like paperwork. If it makes you feel better, Jet hates them too.' Simon peered around the darkened car park as he'd done during their first visit. 'What did you say that prison building was over there? Research and Development? I'd say we give that a try first.'

'As you so accurately pointed out, there's a wall, and a gate. You can't climb over this one, someone's bound to notice.'

'Don't worry, sweetheart, that's why we brought Jet.'

Less than a minute later, Bryce bent down to the complicated security lock. He studied it for a minute, murmured a comment, and extracted a compact tool kit from his pocket. He placed something over his ear and flicked a switch. A powerful beam of light lit up the mechanism.

'Can you open it?' Beth put an arm on his shoulder, bending to see the lock. 'It looks complex.'

Bryce selected an instrument and started to unscrew the cover plate. 'Shouldn't be a problem. This will take some time, kiddies. Talk among yourselves for a while.'

Simon tugged on the ponytail at her neck. 'I won't give up the fight easily.'

Beth peered at him in confusion. 'What?'

'I said I won't give up easily.' Simon gestured to them both.

Beth rose from her crouched position. 'Did I miss something?'

'*We* have something.'

Beth tapped Bryce on the shoulder. 'Do you have any idea what he's talking about?'

'He's an idiot. You'll get used to it. We all had to.' Bryce didn't look up from the lock.

'I know you two have a lot in common.' Simon touched her face. 'You and I, we have chemistry, *real* chemistry. You can't ignore that.'

Beth opened and closed her mouth a couple of times. She stared, and finally put her hands on her hips and fixed him with a confused squint. 'You think—' She paused and started again. 'You think Bryce and I are a *thing*?'

Simon took her by the shoulders. 'Give us a chance, Red. I know I have my faults, but I think we can make this work. Remember how we were together?'

'If you don't mind.' Bryce's tone was pained. 'Could you continue this conversation when I can move to another room, out of earshot? And, by the way, could you keep your voices *down?* In case it's escaped your notice, we're breaking into a secure facility.'

Beth was still trying to form a coherent sentence. 'Simon, we had sex.'

'It wasn't just sex, sweetheart. It meant something.' Simon moved his hands up and down her arms. 'I love you, Dr Elizabeth Barrett.'

Bryce cleared his throat. 'Okay, you know when I said talk among yourselves? I've changed my mind. Could we do the rest of this in silence?'

'You idiot man.' Beth put one hand on Simon's cheek. 'I mean we had *sex*. I don't just have sex with people, especially people I hardly know. Of course it meant something. How could you think otherwise? I don't feel anything romantic for Bryce.' She waved an apologetic hand signal to the agent kneeling before the gate. 'No offence, Bryce.'

'None taken.' Bryce adjusted his lock pick to another angle without looking up.

'It's you.' Beth draped her arms around Simon's neck. 'You crazy, impetuous danger freak, you are the one I had sex with. *You* are the one I'm in love with.'

Simon pulled her closer, trying to read the expression on her face. 'You and Jet have way more in common.'

Beth shook her head. 'Bryce is a friend. Yes, of course, he's gorgeous, intelligent and talented—'

A beam of light illuminated them as Bryce turned his head at her words. 'Thank you, Beth.' Amusement coloured his words.

'Shut up, Jet,' Simon growled at him. 'We're having a moment. Say it again, Red.'

She hugged him tighter. 'I love you.'

Simon grinned and lowered his mouth to hers. His joy was short-lived when a high-pitched beep interrupted them.

Relief was evident in Bryce's voice as he stood and brushed off his trousers. 'Security is down, we're in. And not a *moment* too soon.'

'Lead the way,' Simon gestured to her as they stood flush against the outer wall of the main building.

'Let me get my bearings. I've been here a few times, only in daylight. There.' She pointed to a structure on their right. 'That door should lead to the largest of the research labs. Most of them are joined by corridors between the wings of the building, but that's the main one.'

Bryce bent to the lock. 'If you two want to have sex while I'm doing this, could you kindly move away a few feet so I can't hear?' Beth thumped him on the arm, making him chuckle.

'Why no security guards?' Simon scrutinised the area. 'I was expecting to hog-tie at least one person.'

A low, ominous growl sounded from the distance, giving him the answer. *Bloody Hell, why did I have to ask?* 'We have a problem, Jet. Haden has decided to opt for high-tech locks and low-tech physical security in the form of guard dogs.'

'I'm on it. Give me a few seconds.'

'Speed would be good,' Simon pulled Beth to his side.

'Going as fast as I can.'

Another growl, from a different direction. Both Simon's and Beth's heads swiveled toward the new sound.

'Jet!'

'Quiet, you're not helping.'

Beth shivered in his arms. 'Try to breathe calm and quiet. They're not coming any closer.'

'They don't need to come any closer.' Her voice shook. 'The one on my side is so near I can hear *him* breathing.'

'Almost,' said Bryce. 'Get ready to move, people.'

The lock beeped. Bryce leapt up and barreled through the door, holding it open. The instant the dogs saw movement, they charged. Simon clutched Beth's hand and yanked her through the door after him. Not fast enough. The dog on Beth's left moved like lightning. As she rushed through the door, it latched onto her ankle. Her cry of agony was a knife to his heart.

He caught her under the arms before she hit the ground. His brave scientist used the extra support to kick out with her uninjured foot. The dog yelped in complaint and released its grip, giving Simon the chance to drag her the rest of the way inside. The door slammed behind them, cutting off the insistent barking.

'Dammit.' He lowered her to the ground, cupping her ankle in his hands. 'Bryce, I need light.' His fellow agent was ahead of him, already shining the torch on her lower limb.

Blood oozed from her ankle, soaking through the sock. 'It isn't too bad,' she tried to assure him, even as her voice trembled.

'The hell it isn't.' Simon took off her shoe and peeled back the sock. The cross-trainers had offered some protection, but not enough. Deep puncture wounds around her ankle were bleeding freely.

'This has to be treated.'

'I'll see what I can find.' Bryce took off with the flashlight. The sounds of opening drawers echoed around them.

Simon berated himself for his stupidity. She shouldn't even *be* here. 'Bryce will find a first-aid kit.' He watched her face for signs of shock as he pressed the sock to the worst of the punctures, applying pressure. Beth jerked at the pain without crying out.

Bryce returned empty-handed. 'What sort of a lab doesn't have a first-aid kit?'

'Stay with her. I'll look.' The lab was huge and likely had an entire haul of medical supplies. It was also entirely possible they'd be in the last drawer he opened.

Yanking open one cupboard, he found a large roll of duct tape. 'I know this isn't ideal or even particularly hygienic, but it will keep pressure on the wounds.' He held the bloodied sock in place and bound her foot with the tape.

Alarmed by the pallor of her skin, Simon reached out to touch her face, pulling back before he smeared more blood on her skin. 'We need to get you out of here.'

She shook her head. 'We've come this far. We'll finish this tonight.'

'For god's sake, you're *hurt*.'

'I'm not leaving without evidence. Stop wasting time.'

Surrendering to her stubborn nature, he lifted her into his arms. 'Fifteen minutes and that's it. If we don't find anything, we go.'

'Which way, Beth?' Bryce shone the light around the room.

Beth closed her eyes. 'Hold on, let me think. Okay, there should be a door to a corridor next to a 3D printer, go about fifty feet then branch left...wait, I mean right.'

'You're doing great, sweetheart.' Simon kept close behind Bryce, following her concise directions to the letter.

'You're looking for a room with floor to ceiling glass walls and a blue door. It had lots of storage cupboards, black ones. *There*, I think that's it.'

Bryce took care of the lock, holding up his hand to forestall them while he checked for secondary alarms. Once inside, Simon lowered her to one of the office chairs in the cramped, dimly lit room. 'Point. We'll do the moving around.'

One by one they searched every drawer, every cabinet. Bryce was the one who found the cloth in a locked cupboard. He turned it over in his hands, examining the tight weave and the light weight. 'Incredible.'

'Yes, as long as you don't need to store it in the heat for any length of time. Just let me check this cabinet and then we go.' Simon opened another cupboard as big as a wardrobe. Inside he saw the same textile fashioned into something familiar.

'I was right.' He pulled out the tactical vest. 'Bryce, look at this.'

Bryce came over. 'Only three layers of textile, no wonder it's so light. This is roughly made, obviously a prototype.'

Simon slipped the vest over his shoulders, fastening the snaps. He twisted and turned his body. 'Feels just like coarse linen. We'll take this as well.'

Bryce lowered his voice. 'Beth is hurt. How exactly do you plan to get out of here?'

'I can carry her. We'll make a run for the same door we entered.'

Bryce shook his head. 'Those dogs have a taste of blood now. They'll charge us as soon as we try to leave the building.'

'There must be another exit. This place is too big for just one door. It's just a matter of finding the others.'

'There's a high probability of finding more guard dogs as well.'

A slamming door had Simon pivoting towards the sound, whipping the gun from its holster. Bryce echoed his action.

'Wait, *wait!*' Beth stumbled from the chair, hands waving. 'Put those away, this is my lab assistant, remember?'

Bryce lowered his weapon, Simon didn't. 'What are you doing here?'

Tim had his hands in the air. He stepped further into the room, his worried gaze flickering between the three of them. 'Working.'

'At this time of night?' The question came from Bryce.

'It's a new job, I'm falling behind. I heard a noise and I came to investigate, that's all.' The words were blurted out.

'It's okay, don't worry.' Beth tried to hobble toward him, before giving up and regaining her seat.

'What are you doing here, Dr Barrett?'

'Tim, you need to listen to me. I know this is going to sound crazy and it's a lot to take in, but the textile is faulty. I think Haden Corp has been trying to sabotage my research to cover it up.' Beth took a deep breath, the calm, placating tone of her voice beginning to slip. 'They've been trying to kill me.'

'A difficult task, as it turns out. Apparently, you have more lives than a cat.' The words seemed to reverberate around the room.

Simon swiveled to the new threat, the gun steady in his hand, to see the head of Haden Laboratories standing on the other side of the glass wall.

Haden gestured to him and Bryce and their drawn weapons. 'You may as well put those away, gentlemen. This glass is completely bulletproof.' His voice carried easily through the intercom. 'And the door is now locked.' He waved the keys in his hand.

With a sinking in the pit of his stomach, Simon stole a look at Bryce for confirmation. His colleague shook his head. They'd been so concerned with speed, Bryce hadn't disabled the lock after entering.

'How did you know we were here?' Simon asked.

'Your technical friend there is extremely clever.' Haden indicated Bryce. 'I wouldn't have guessed for one moment the outer locks could be breached. You missed one thing, though. There are pressure sensors on the floor. You tripped them when you entered.'

'Why come here yourself in the middle of the night?' Bryce asked. 'Why not just send the police?'

Haden gestured to Beth. 'Our lovely Elizabeth already knows the answer to that, don't you? After all, you just told Tim we were trying to kill you. We don't *really* want the police involved yet. Afterwards, when we clarify our story, they'll be brought in.'

'You hired those men, didn't you?' Beth's voice shook with anger. 'The ones I saw outside my house and at the awards night.'

Haden lifted one shoulder in a shrug. 'Believe it or not, they did come highly recommended, a fact I now dispute as they were obviously totally incapable of doing the job they were hired to do. How difficult is it to kill one woman and one bodyguard?' He laughed, a cruel, brittle sound. 'As I said, Beth, you have more lives than a cat.'

'Why?' Beth's voice shook. 'Make me understand what was so important that I had to *die*.'

Simon and Bryce glanced at each other. Simon was happy to keep Haden's attention on Beth for as long as possible until they finalised a plan. Bulletproof glass had one advantage. It meant bullets couldn't get in or out.

'Money,' Haden replied. 'You must understand it isn't anything personal. It's just money. I gather you already figured out the textile is useless after extended exposure to heat. We estimate one to two years' degradation time under normal circumstances. Plenty of time to make our fortune through military contracts. If you had only stuck to our testing procedures, my dear Dr Barrett. We chose you so very carefully.'

'Wh–what do you mean?'

Another brittle laugh. Simon's fingers curled into a fist.

'My sweet little Beth. With your old-fashioned microscope and your award for mould.' The last word was said with derision. 'Did you think we hired you for your skill? No, my dear, we hired you for your reputation, your *spotless* reputation. Quiet, unassuming, methodical. You were our perfect cover. No one would suspect you as corrupt until it was too late. Once your reputation was in ruins we could easily discard your research, blame you for the failure of our product.' He tapped a finger to his lips. 'Independent laboratories, how very clever of you. And secretive.'

'How did you even know?'

'One of your hand-written notes on results came to my attention. It didn't fit the pre-arranged testing schedule and sent me on a path to investigate further. Although I was unable to find any solid data of this extracurricular testing after the fire, when you came to my office your interesting comment on the subject of independent labs confirmed my suspicions. You had damning evidence, I was certain of it. Who knew what else you had secreted away? You can see why you had to die a little earlier than we originally planned.'

A chill ran along Simon's spine. Haden was giving away a lot of information. The question was why?

'Eventually, it'll be obvious the textile does degrade. Soldiers will start to die,' Beth said. 'How will you explain that?'

Haden shrugged 'That is the beauty of it. We won't have to. As I said, we will have made all our money by then. We will blame the initial testing procedures. In other words, blame you. You got mixed up with the wrong people and died for it.' Haden's tone was matter of fact now, even cordial. 'The pretty little scientist with the lovely red hair and the lovely green eyes secretly dealing in drugs. Your spotless reputation was a lie and your testing procedures shoddy.'

Beth's eyes blazed with fury as if the threat to her scientific reputation was more important than someone trying to kill her. 'How *dare* you? How dare you take my work and my ethics and throw it away for *money*.'

Haden's attention was all on Beth now. Bryce nudged Simon, with a flick of his head he indicated the phone hidden behind his back. Bryce was texting one-handed at high speed. *Code red. Send a team. Haden Corp Main Labs.* He'd added the address and the exact location of the room. His colleague wasn't one to leave out important details, even when texting blind.

'We did think of offering you a bribe.' Haden was still talking. 'The trouble is, we realised early on you were annoyingly incorruptible. We knew even if we explained our situation and offered you a large pile of money, you would simply report us to the authorities. As you can see, we had no choice. You had to be disposed of.'

Simon peeked at Bryce and frowned. Something wasn't right. Haden was too calm, too confident. A faint buzzing noise made him look down. Bryce angled the phone behind his back so Simon could see the message on the screen. *Ten minutes.* That was it. Two simple words, but they sent a rush of relief through his body. Simon held up one hand just high enough to draw Bryce's attention and splayed his fingers once, twice. Bryce nodded.

'What happens now?' Beth asked.

'As I said, you were obviously incorruptible. Fortunately for us, not everyone is.' Haden smiled, killing Simon's momentary relief. He grasped the horrifying truth a moment too late. The real danger was already inside the room.

Tim pulled a gun from under his lab coat, aimed it at Beth, and fired.

Simon reacted on instinct. He leapt, throwing himself in front of her.

Pain.

Beth screamed his name. The sound seemed to come from a long way off. Simon heard more shots. For some reason, they didn't hurt.

'Simon, oh my god, Simon. Bryce, please, *please.*'

The last thing Simon remembered was Beth's hands on him and terror in her voice.

Before everything went blissfully dark.

Chapter 7

Simon opened his eyes, his mind instantly awake. His body was a different matter, muscle and bone were sluggish and uncooperative.

First things first. He conceivably wasn't dead. Judging from the amount of white assaulting his eyes, he would guess his current location to be a hospital, or else heaven was *annoyingly* bright. He squinted until his pupils adjusted, then opened them again with more success.

He peered around the room, hoping to see a tall redhead. Instead, he spied Bryce lounging in one of the visitors' chairs, legs crossed at the ankles, reading some sort of electronics magazine.

'Jet? What the bloody hell happened? Where is she? Where's Red?'

Bryce didn't look up from his article. 'Stop calling me Jet or I'll shoot you. Oh, wait, someone beat me to it.'

'*Jet*,' he emphasised the word with unconcealed irritation. 'Sarcasm does not become you. Where's Red?'

'Beth is fine,' Bryce cut him off, finally pulling his attention from the magazine. 'Some idiot with limited surgical knowledge put about a mile of duct tape on her foot. Oh, wait. That was you.' His fellow agent appeared to be enjoying himself. 'A medical professional is currently doing a much better job of dealing with her injury. If it makes you feel better, it took a long time for them to convince her to leave the room. They started to use words like "foot amputation" to scare her into going with them.'

Simon smiled. *That's my girl.* He stretched, the instinctive move curtailed by a sudden sharp pain in his upper chest. 'Did we get the bad guys?'

'All locked up and accounted for.' Bryce had resumed his reading. 'You want the cliff notes or the whole saga?'

'Just talk.' Simon bit the words out.

'The team arrived, stormed the lab, Haden tried to run, they caught him in the car park. The corrupt lab assistant should consider himself lucky. Beth launched herself at him with considerable ferocity after he shot you.'

Simon sucked in a pained breath when he remembered seeing the gun raised, realising Tim's intention. 'What happened to him?'

'I believe he's across the hall with a head wound.'

'Red did that?'

'No, I shot him.'

'I see.' *It's always the quiet ones.* 'Thank you.'

Bryce turned the page. 'You're welcome. He was trying to hurt Beth, I had no choice. You're lucky, the prototype vest hadn't been heat tested. You have some intense bruising, but it did stop the bullet that would have hit your heart and killed you. It's a shame the first bullet missed the textile and got your shoulder, otherwise you would have gotten off much more lightly. That sample vest wasn't made for someone of your unnaturally huge size.'

'Insults? I'm in pain, and you give me insults?' Simon decided to risk some movement. Lying flat on his back was making his spine ache. He tried to raise himself up to a partly sitting position.

'There's a message from Jared on your phone.'

'Concern for my welfare?' Simon reached out and snagged it from the bedside table.

'No, it's about your new goddaughter Marie.'

The photo on the small screen showed a beaming Cecilia holding a pink-wrapped newborn.

'Cecilia went into labour shortly after hearing you'd been shot. Jared is blaming you for the early arrival, so I suggest a low profile for a while.'

Simon chuckled, and after replacing the phone, he tried once again to sit up.

'What are you *doing*?' Beth yelled at him from the doorway, hobbling toward him with the use of a cane. 'Stay right there, you idiot. You got shot! You can't go moving around.'

He drank in the sight of her, from the disheveled red hair to those stunning emerald eyes, flashing at him in anger and concern. 'Good morning, sweetheart. Wait, is it morning? I've lost track of time.'

'Lay back, just lay back. Don't try to cuddle me, Simon. You've been shot.'

He ignored her and reached up to snag an arm around her neck even though it hurt. 'Kiss me first, then you can yell at me. I need your lips on mine. I got shot, I need a reward.'

Bryce folded his magazine and stood. 'That's my cue to leave.'

Beth kissed him and then threw her arms around his neck, being careful of his injury, and buried her head in his neck. It took him a moment to realise she was crying.

'Hey, sweetheart, it's okay. I haven't spoken to a doctor, but I'm pretty sure I'm going to live.'

She shook her head without looking at him.

'I'm *not* going to live? Christ, that's a shock. How long do I have?'

The teasing worked and she raised a tear-stained face to him. 'No, I mean, yes. You're going to be fine. I was so scared, Simon. Don't you *ever* do that to me again.'

He kissed her, a reassuring brush of lips over hers. 'I promise, and I'm unlikely to have a choice. Jared has this rule about agents taking on dangerous missions once they get hitched. I can see myself as a trainer though. I detest the paperwork side of things, but martial arts training perhaps? Unarmed combat training? I could do that.'

She peered at him in confusion. 'Do you have a concussion?'

He answered the question with another kiss, because the touch of her mouth was the most important thing in the world right now. She could catch up on the other stuff later, once she understood he wasn't going anywhere. 'Climb up here.'

'Simon, I can't.'

'Come on.' He gave her his most winning smile. 'I need a cuddle, and you won't let me get out of bed. Apparently, I've been shot.'

The metal cane clattered to the floor as she manoeuvred her body onto the narrow bed.

'Leave it.' He pulled her closer. 'You don't need it. If I'm stuck in this bed, you can be stuck with me.'

There were a few thousand ways he needed to say I love you. Romantic ways. Simon could do romantic. He was exceptionally good at romantic and looked forward to wooing her properly without the constant threat of danger that had chased them since they first met.

For the moment he was content to have her cuddled up beside him even though the painkillers in his system were making their presence known and pulling him back under.

Plenty of time.

Beth sighed. 'I can't go to sleep here.'

'Why not? Jet will keep everyone away. He has his uses.'

'You're impossible.'

Simon surrendered to a yawn wide enough to make his jaw crack. 'I know. People tell me that all the time.'

She snuggled closer. Simon held her safe and secure in his arms and surrendered to healing sleep.

༶

Beth woke up with a start when she moved and her bandaged foot struck the end of the hard hospital bed.

Taking deep breaths until the throbbing subsided, she watched the sleeping man beside her.

His blond hair was messy, his face pale. Lines bracketed his mouth as if he was still in pain, even asleep. Thick, dark lashes framed the dark smudges under his eyes. Her poor protector looked vulnerable and wounded. Beth traced his cheek with her fingers, brushed a curl away from his forehead. Had it only been a week? Could such strong feelings develop in such a short time? Her life had been quiet and orderly until Simon Winters flew into it with all the ferocity of a winter's storm. Beth smiled at her inadvertent play on words.

'It isn't rational,' she murmured. 'And I don't care. You mean so much to me.'

'Good.'

Beth yelped at his unexpected response. 'You're supposed to be asleep.'

Simon's lips curled upward, even though his eyes remained closed. 'I am asleep. I'm dreaming a beautiful scientist is touching me and saying she loves me.'

'I didn't actually say that.'

'I'm paraphrasing.' The dark lashes lifted. 'I meant what I said outside Haden's Laboratory, Beth, I do love you.'

'You called me Beth. Normally that means we're in danger.'

Simon laughed then winced. 'Don't make me laugh. It jiggles parts of me that hurt. How's your ankle?'

'Sore. I hit it on the bedframe.'

'My poor love.' Simon lifted his arm then winced again. 'Damn, we're a fine pair, aren't we? Both injured. At least we're in the right place. I've been dying –

figuratively speaking – to get you back in bed with me, preferably one a little bigger.'

'I do love you too,' she blurted out. 'I know it isn't logical, but I do.'

'Logic is overrated. Tell me again. Kiss me if you like.'

'We're not very private.'

'I don't care in the least.'

Beth twisted her upper body until she could reach the spare blanket folded on the side table. She shook it out. The end caught Simon's phone and she grabbed it before the device hit the floor. The screen flashed to life and Beth saw the beaming face of Cecilia and the precious bundle in her arms.

'Oh, Cecilia had the baby.'

'Yes, apparently Jared is blaming me.'

'For the conception?'

Simon burst out laughing, which ended in a strangled gasp. 'Ouch. Please don't tell Jared you had that thought. He'll chop me into little pieces. Sweetheart, what *are* you doing with that thing?'

Beth finally had the blanket open, and she spread it out, pulling the stiff utilitarian cotton over their heads. 'Barrett World.'

'Ah, Barrett World, my favourite place.'

The harsh lights of the hospital room dimmed to a murky grey under the much-washed covering. But it was private. Beth wanted private.

Simon shifted his weight, groaning as he tried to get comfortable. 'Distract me from this pain. Tell me what's happening.'

'I've become insanely popular. My phone is full up with messages. I swear everyone I've ever met wants all the dirty little details. I'll deal with them later.'

'Have the press been hassling you? I'm still under contract as your protector, remember.'

'It'll all over the news. Jade is handling that side of things. I don't want to talk to them, not now, preferably not ever. I did hear from The Scientific Institute. They're mortified over their assumption of my guilt and want to know how they can make it up to me.'

'What did you say?'

'I want a trophy to go with my certificate. A flashy bauble.'

That made him grin, as she knew it would. 'I *am* rubbing off on you.'

'Only in small doses. Don't get cocky. Cecilia sent a lovely message even though she must have been in labour at the time. I can't believe she was thinking of me.'

'She's a special woman. We should have one.'

'A special woman?'

'A baby.'

She eye-rolled him at the abrupt change of subject. 'People don't just *have* babies. That sort of thing takes careful planning and time.'

'Tell that to my new goddaughter. I assure you there was very little planning involved in her creation. Ask Cecilia, she'll admit it.'

Somehow they'd gone from 'I love you' to having babies in one swoop. Simon's spontaneity was something she'd need to get used to. Snuggling closer, she kissed him, running her fingers through his hair. 'Thank you.'

'For what?'

'Everything.' She hesitated over the next words. 'I think I should give up my work. You heard what Haden said. I'm not very good at it.'

Simon yanked her against him, ignoring the pain the movement obviously caused. Even in their murky hideaway, his eyes were flashing with anger. 'Don't you *dare* listen to what he said. You're extraordinary, brilliant. I will drag you to your laboratory every day and make you work if that's what it takes to convince you.'

Tears pricked her eyes at his faith in her. Her reply was husky with them. 'I don't have a lab any more, or a car for that matter. And I don't even think my house holds the same appeal as it did.'

'Good. Move into mine. I'll buy you another car, and a lab if you want one.'

His determined words made her giggle. 'We always have the strangest conversations when we're in Barrett World. The car was expensive. I spent all of Haden's advance money on it. I'll never be able to afford another one. Maybe if I sell the house and buy something smaller?'

'I mean it, Red, I'll buy you a new Ferrari and a new house if you decide you don't want to live with me, but you should. I'm a superb cook.'

Beth tapped his chest. 'You're rambling.'

'It's only the truth. I am a superb cook. And I *will* buy you a dozen cars, a dozen houses, a dozen labs. Not sure what you'll do with a dozen labs though.'

Something about the intensity of his words made her take notice. She rose up on one elbow. 'Simon, are you rich?'

'Yes. Does that bother you?'

Beth scowled at the surprisingly simple answer. 'You mean you have money because agents are paid well?'

'They are. I had a head start with my parents.'

She nibbled on her lip, memories coming to the fore. His townhouse in Mayfair. The sleek black sports car. His rich, upper-class accent.

'Where do your parents live?'

'Depends on the time of year. My mother loves to ski, so Switzerland is high on the list during the snow season. They both stick to the estate in spring and autumn.'

Estate? *I grew up in an old house*, his throw away words came back to her. 'When was your parents' house built?'

'Fifteen hundreds, sixteen hundreds, I told you it's old.'

'You mean it's *Elizabethan*?'

'That's what I said, old.'

She chuckled. 'You're not noble, are you? You know, with an aristocratic title.'

He lifted her hand and played with her fingers.

'Simon?'

'I don't use it. It does come in handy for restaurant reservations.'

She stared at him, aware her mouth had dropped open and unable to do anything about it. Bryce had referred to him as Sir Simon when they first met. *Sir Simon Winters?*

Simon kissed the tips of her fingers, still talking. 'I have to warn you, my mother will expect a big wedding. My sister Olivia had about five hundred at hers. If that's too much, we can always elope. I have an apartment in Manhattan. It's a great place to escape to. Red, honey, are you listening to me?'

I'm in love with a secret agent who's obscenely rich and some sort of lord. Beth began to giggle.

'Red?' Simon peered at her in alarm. 'How many painkillers did they give you? Are you all right? Look at me. How many fingers am I holding up? Do I need to call the nurse?'

She laughed harder, unable to hold back until Simon tried to sit up. The blanket threatened to dislodge, and Beth yanked it back into place. Then she pushed him down, lest he hurt himself. 'You reckless, adorable, gorgeous, crazy, danger-seeking maniac. What on earth am I going to do with you?'

'Love me?'

'You better believe it.' She kissed him.

Perfection was such an elegant word. Simon Winters was her own personal perfection, in their own unique world.

Barrett World.

Where he belonged.

Thank You

Thank you for reading *Passion in Flames*.

We hope you enjoyed it.

If you enjoyed it, please consider leaving an honest review on Goodreads or Amazon. Reviews can help readers find books and we would be grateful for your help. Thank you for taking the time to let others know what you thought.

This book is Book 2 in the Love Under Fire series, published by Serenity Press under its Serenity Romance imprint.

To see more stories from the Love Under Fire series or other Serenity Press publications, visit serenitypress.org

About the author

Carolyn Wren is a Perth-based author whose family travelled a great deal during her early life, giving her a fascination with the world around her.

Her eleven books have been nominated for twelve national and international writing awards, resulting in five winners' trophies.

Carolyn doesn't limit herself to one sub-genre of romance, preferring to let her characters take control. The end results can range from light hearted, sweet comedic contemporary, through to sexy, action-packed romantic suspense and emotion driven urban fantasy.

She is a movie buff who takes great joy in watching stories as well as writing them.

CPSIA information can be obtained
at www.ICGtesting.com
Printed in the USA
LVHW041240301219
642052LV00002B/284